NETWORK OF
DECEPTION

A NOVEL

SPENCER E.
MOSES

Revell

a division of Baker Publishing Group
Grand Rapids, Michigan

© 2014 by Spencer E. Moses

Published by Revell
a division of Baker Publishing Group
P.O. Box 6287, Grand Rapids, MI 49516-6287
www.revellbooks.com

Printed in the United States of America

Library of Congress Cataloging-in-Publication Data
Moses, Spencer E.
    Network of deception : a novel / Spencer E. Moses.
      pages cm
    ISBN 978-0-8007-2256-2 (pbk.)
    1. Information warfare—Fiction. 2. International relations—Fiction.
3. Suspense fiction. I. Title.
PS3613.O77933N48 2014
813'.6—dc23   2014005585

The author is represented by and this book is published in association with the literary
agency of WordServe Literary Group, Ltd., www.wordserveliterary.com.

14 15 16 17 18 19 20   7 6 5 4 3 2 1

ACKNOWLEDGMENTS

Our friends are priceless and always deeply appreciated. My agent Greg Johnson remains one of those friends who is forever prized. A better editor than Vicki Crumpton none can find. Thanks also to Dana Collins and Ramona Hanson for their proofreading and responses.

PROLOGUE

OCTOBER 2, 1991

The wind picked up, blowing a thin cloud of dust over the bleak Israeli field that provided a cemetery for the kibbutz. Red poppies clustered around small grave markers sticking up out of the grass, silent reminders of long-gone friends and ancestors. In the middle of the grassy plot, dirt had been piled beside a black hole in the ground. A crowd of people stood quietly with their heads bowed, saying nothing. The scent of freshly dug dirt filled young Simone Koole's nose. With her arm around Alona, her mother, Simone supported her like a pillar of granite. Her mother leaned into Simone lest she fall at any moment. Alona carried her own overflowing load of past tragedies, but today added an unbearable weight to the burden.

A woman who lived on Kibbutz Shalom came over and hugged Alona and then squeezed Simone's hand. Nothing was said. Silence served its own purpose best. In the distance,

Simone could hear the men trudging toward the cemetery. She didn't want to hear the cadence, but she couldn't make their feet stop beating out the dirge that mourned the end of a precious life.

For a moment, Simone considered jumping into the grave. She wasn't sure how life could ever go on from this day.

"Bless you, my dears," old Mendel Kapel said to Simone and Alona. "The Holy One bless you." He tugged at his long gray bread and trudged away.

Old Mendel Kapel had always been one of the community. One of her earliest memories was of him warning her about the Palestinian terrorists. They would cut the throats of children if given the chance. She didn't know much more than this fact, but it was enough to make her tremble.

Simone had lived in the kibbutz all her life and been nothing more than one of the kids. They were one big happy family, wanting little more than to till the lands, laugh together at meals, sleep in warm beds at night, and protect each other from the marauders who attacked in the dark or shot rifles clandestinely from behind the large trees that bordered the fields.

The men in their village had always called her Little Miss Bright Eyes. Her long black hair and suntanned skin made her one of the joys of the community. Because Simone always stayed happy, they sometimes thought of her as a good-luck charm. At mealtime in the great hall, she often ate with other families who laughed at her little jokes and funny stories. Life had been hard but good. Good until now, when the word *good* had disappeared from her vocabulary.

The tramping of men's feet grew louder, and Simone

tensed. They would be here any minute and she'd have to watch. She would have to for no other reason than to help maintain her mother's stability. Jewish people lived knowing the inevitability of death, but when it was someone dear to you, the promise of eternity no longer comforted. Death became the ultimate, deplorable enemy.

"Here they come," Alona whispered to Simone and clutched her hand even more tightly.

With the afternoon sun shining brightly over their fields, the six men marched up the road with the long narrow box dangling from rope handles held by these longtime acquaintances of the deceased. Two men wore black fedoras; the rest kept their small prayer caps fixed on the top of their heads. Their beards wound down from their chins, only adding to their forlorn appearance. Each man's eyes carried a sober, red cast. Halting next to the large hole, they set their burden down carefully.

The rabbi began chanting a prayer. Simone could no longer hear his words. Her heart and mind had drifted away. She loved her father with all her heart. Jokin Koole had never been the tallest man in the kibbutz, but he was stout and everyone knew Jokin had unusual strength. After his parents died in the Warsaw uprising, he had escaped the Nazi terror and immigrated to Israel.

Jokin and Alona met at the kibbutz and began the rigorous life required to survive with so little. In time, the kibbutz prospered and their small house became the home Simone grew up in.

She had fiercely loved her father because he was so good to her. At night, he always tucked her in bed and asked her questions about her day. Jokin loved hearing Simone describe her favorite doll and what they had done that afternoon. He laughed at her stories and chuckled when she described her antics in the big barn where they kept the horses. Simone loved to crawl in and out of the stalls, spending hours brushing a horse's coat and piling hay. Even the workhorses seemed to understand her words. Jokin admired that trait and told her so often.

He would tell her that they rejoiced because they were free. Jews had their own land, their own state. Often his monologues would turn into speeches praising *Adonai* for providing such a paradise for them. Certainly, they had to work hard, but that was good for them. Hard work made healthy people. Hard work produced endurance, endurance produced a noble character, and a noble character made for a long life. Every morning they began the day with the *Modeh Ani* followed by other prayers and then finally the recitation of the *Shema Yisrael* and the prayers of blessing that followed. Never again would her father say these prayers with her.

The men began lowering Jokin's simple casket into the ground. Once the pine box rested on the bottom, the rabbi nodded to the *minyan*. The ten men indicated they understood. Simone picked up a handful of dirt and sprinkled it lightly on the top of the casket. Alona didn't move. Finally, she dropped a small amount of dirt as was her duty. A pallbearer picked up a shovel and threw dirt into the hole. The men and women of the kibbutz began filling the grave. Each shovelful of dirt bounced off the casket with a thud, but the sound only sparked a new sense of resolution within Simone. She would put away her little girl ways. No longer would she be Little Miss Bright Eyes. With each load of dirt crashing against the casket, her determination grew stronger. Her childhood intentions to find a nice man to marry and toil the fields together until death parted them began to fade. She would spend her life fighting the murderers who slipped in during the night and killed innocent people.

One by one, the members of the kibbutz walked past the dark hole. Some threw in dirt; others took the shovel and pitched in larger amounts. Simone watched, staring into the grave with resolute intensity.

The rabbi's final prayers spilled out at a routine pace. One word followed another with a rhythm that moved as if directed by a conductor. Simone could almost see an invisible hand waving back and forth to keep the rabbi in sync. She had to think of such things to keep her grief from sweeping her away.

Old Rabbi Cohen usually never touched women, but he stopped when he walked past Simone and Alona. With a tear in his eye, he bit his lip. He made one gentle tap on their clutched hands and then walked to the head of the oblong hole in the ground.

"Our brother Jokin's soul will forever abide with the martyrs of our people," the rabbi said. "We will remember him always as a man of great courage and an indomitable force in this kibbutz. The Holy One, blessed be his name, will smile on him. We can rejoice in the reception that his soul will receive in paradise."

The time had come to put gentleness aside. She must take on the strength of her father. His courage to walk out in an open field and work even when danger lurked nearby must

11

become hers as well. Never again would she retreat from danger; she would face the assault fearlessly. She would stand against the brutality regardless of the cost.

The rabbi lowered his *siddur*, his prayer book. The last shovelful of dirt had finished the mound over Jokin Koole. The wind blustered again. Silence settled over the cemetery.

"I must go home," Alona said. "I cannot stand to see more."

"There is no shame in that," Simone said. "But I must stay longer."

The crowd slowly dispersed, but she didn't move.

"Go rest, Simone," the rabbi said. "No one can sustain such an experience for long."

"Thank you. I will go shortly."

Once again, the old man uncharacteristically patted her on the shoulder and walked away. No one else seemed to want to say more. The crowd drifted back to the kibbutz. Finally, Simone stood alone. The wind picked up, and dust blew from the top of the grave. The damp smell of earth was replaced by a hint of jasmine drifting in from the field. In the solitude of the cemetery, Simone felt a strength bubbling up within her that seemed to rise up out of the ground beneath her. It felt like an assurance that her father and all the other ancestors who had lived through such terrible atrocities would be with her no matter where her path took her. The more difficult the task, the more she could know they stood in the shadows.

In that moment, Simone knew what she must do.

1

The snowcapped mountains beyond Tehran, Iran, stood against a dark blue sky. After weeks of unrest caused by rioting, calm once more settled over the sprawling city. The minarets had sounded the call to prayer earlier in the morning, and traffic had picked up across the city. The ruling mullahs had finished their discussion of the day's business and come to agreement on the route Iran should take in the coming months. Each religious leader had expressed a varying opinion, but in the end they all agreed on what must follow. As the conversations ceased, they summoned Ebrahim Jalili, the newly elected president of Iran. Guards opened the door, and the president walked in briskly.

Wearing his usual light brown suit and white shirt with no tie, he bowed to the six men seated in a semicircle in gold chairs. Each man wore the usual circular turban and robe expected of his office. They scrutinized Jalili with such intensity that the president could almost feel a burning sensation. Jalili bowed to each mullah, already knowing the religious leaders were not interested in his opinions. No chair was offered to the president. He was there to receive orders, not share ideas.

The Supreme Leader, Ayatollah Ali Hashemi, raised his hand in a gesture that looked like a blessing, when in fact he was signaling that a pronouncement was about to be made.

"The attempted coup in June has been defeated by the Revolutionary Guard. Your election is secure, and we do not expect more demonstrations. If problems should occur, the detractors are to be dealt with quickly and harshly. Do you understand?"

The president bowed his head and nodded.

"We want you to make overtures to Syria. It is our considered opinion that the Syrians will prove to be our best and strongest allies in the region. With their assistance, we will be able to steadily move toward dominance in the entire region. You are to court their needs and provide any help required. We may well need their assistance if we are to crush Israel."

"Should I be concerned about an American response to these efforts?" Ebrahim Jalili asked.

"We must be cautious with the American infidels. These dogs of disaster have not forgotten that we occupied their embassy some years ago." The Supreme Leader pointed his finger at the president. "As I recall, you were part of that takeover."

For the first time, Jalili smiled. "Yes."

The Supreme Leader continued, "We have no doubt the Americans are watching our every move and attempting to monitor our nuclear technology. We cannot afford to allow them to get a stranglehold on our efforts to achieve nuclear capacity. They will not retreat from a policy of containment. You understand what I am saying?"

Once again, the president nodded. "Yes, sir."

"We have centrifuges that enrich uranium," the ayatollah said. "As you know, increasing the number and speed of the machines will increase the level of our capacity to make a nuclear device that would wipe out Israel. We want you to proceed with this effort regardless of what the West does."

"I expect we will face increased sanctions," Jalili said.

"So be it," Hashemi answered. "Once we have a nuclear device, no one can stand in our way. We will once again be the dominant power, and Islam can conquer the world without the impediment of the Jew swine and their economic props, the Americans."

"I have concerns that our people will revolt against the sting of economic sanctions," the president said. "We may face a backlash."

"I will expect you to control any such issue," the ayatollah said with a condescending twist in his voice. "Such is your job."

Ebrahim Jalili winced but said nothing.

"Your offices must keep a close eye out for Jewish spies. Don't underestimate their abilities."

"We will not," Jalili assured him. "Is there anything more that I should be aware of?"

"Not at this time," Ayatollah Hashemi said. "We will expect results."

2

Simone Koole had paused by the sandstone monument each time she walked to work on Tel Aviv's King Saul Boulevard. Dedicated to the agents who had fallen in secret, the monument held special meaning to those who could disappear in a similar fashion. Simone kept walking. Mossad's office facilities stood innocuously simple and plain. No signs, placards, or memorials marked the entrance to the most feared intelligence agency in the world. Called "the Office" by operatives, the center was a self-contained building inside of an outer shell with a self-sufficient source of energy and water. In case of a national attack, Mossad would keep running. There were other, more secret entrances, but Simone Koole usually entered through the front door because she preferred a daily walk rather than driving her car.

Director Dar Dagan's office occupied part of the top floor. With windows on all sides, the Mossad executive director's office had a commanding view of the city and the harbor. Dagan was highly efficient and didn't make mistakes. His predecessor had fallen on hard times following the last Lebanon invasion that ended in more of a stalemate than a victory. Simone understood Dagan wouldn't make the same mistakes.

Simone punched her identity card into the elevator's slot and started up. She thought about Dagan's request to see her first thing this morning. His line of questioning would be tough as usual because the man caught every detail. Simone liked the fact that he kept the country well protected and ensured no one would have to face the kind of people who killed her father.

The elevator door opened. Dagan's secretary glared at Simone as if she might be an escaped convict or smuggling a load of plastic explosives.

"I'm here to see Dagan," Simone said.

"He's waiting for you," the secretary said without batting an eye or changing her expression.

Simone knocked once and turned the handle. Dagan sat in a short-sleeved white shirt, looking as if he might breathe fire any minute. "Sit down," he said. "We need to talk."

Simone tried to look calm with a touch of indifference. To do otherwise would be to suggest intimidation, and Dar Dagan hated fear. She sat down slowly. "Hello, dragon man."

"I wish you would stop calling me that." Dagan picked up a file and thumbed through it. "You've been crossing swords with the GID boys again," he said. "The General Intelligence Department of the Saudi intelligence service remembers you well, I'm sure."

Simone nodded.

"They scare you?"

She shook her head.

Dagan abruptly laughed. "You're a tough nut to crack,

Simone." He relit the stub of a cigar that he might have been smoking off and on for a couple of days and blew the acrid-smelling smoke into the air. "Well, the GID boys seem to think you're a real John Wayne. You might remember the hit in Dubai where the senior Hamas military commander Mahmourd al-Mabhoub got knocked off in an Arab Emirates hotel. Everyone said that it was a Mossad job and thought you'd had some part in interrogating al-Mabhoub before he got the ax. What do you have to say about that?"

"No comment." Simone smiled.

"All right, then. We're still running Operation Damocles in Egypt. Our people have located one rocket scientist hiding in Giza. One isn't enough. I want you to look into that job and see what else can be done."

Simone pulled out a pad and made a note.

"Your experience with the Arabs will be important for this matter in Egypt. I've now put it on your plate."

"Consider it handled." She started to get up from her chair.

"Sit down. There's another little problem. The Iranians are doing everything in their power to become the dominant force in the Middle East, including trying to destabilize Saudi Arabia."

"We're paying close attention to this situation," Simone said.

"Yeah? Well, they've got a uranium enrichment program and they're on the way to making a nuclear bomb."

"You never authorized me to bomb them." Simone returned his serve with the smoothness of a Wimbledon tennis champion. "Besides, I didn't think walking into their Natanz plant with bombs strapped under my arms would wreck enough of their centrifuges."

Dagan lifted an eyebrow. "Well, we now have a big problem. They've got 984 of those machines going full tilt. International sanctions haven't slowed them down. We're talking about nuclear capacity in a short time."

"I've seen the reports. And we've seen the likes of their new president before," Simone said. "If they get the bomb, we're the target."

"That's my assessment as well," Dagan said. "We have to do something and do it now. We can't bomb them. We have to be more subtle. More devastating."

"What would you suggest, sir?"

"I want an alternative to the use of nuclear weapons on Iran. I want you to find an aggressive way to attack this problem without the big blast. Maybe the Americans will help us, but we can't count on it. We certainly can't use their government to get at this problem. You'll need to find another way to get going without Washington. Keep the US government out of the project. Got it?"

Simone nodded but knew Dagan had just assigned her an almost impossible task. "Almost" could drive a person insane.

"Tell the agents under you to pay attention to Egypt. The Muslim Brotherhood might be playing games. We believe they want to kill Egypt's peace treaty with us. Even Gamal Abdel Nasser banned these nutcases before they could take over the state."

"I know their history," Simone said. "The radicals are the true sons of Iran's mullahs. Nothing would please them more than a good old-fashioned revolution. I've got the picture.

But I think you're telling me that the number one objective is to stop Iran from making the Big Bomb."

"Absolutely. You know how they think. I want you to hit them hard."

"While I'm at it, do you want me to find a cure for cancer?"

"Don't get smart with me, Simone. I'm deadly serious. Get after it."

Simone settled back in her chair. Mossad had trained her to be an agent of superb skill. She was an expert in martial arts, and her marksmanship was unequaled. Her physical condition surpassed that of many men. But taking on the problem of Iran was a tall order.

Dagan stood up and took off his glasses. As he cleaned them slowly, she could tell he was studying her face and trying to shift into a more resolved appearance.

"I know this assignment is difficult," Dagan said. "Highly demanding. We both know what happens when the fence falls down."

Simone thought of her father. She could only tighten her lips.

"Every resource will be at your disposal. Now, go do your job."

Simone stood up slowly. Without saying another word, she turned and walked out of the room.

3

During the eighteen years since its inception, the Conundrum organization had been more successful than Eric Stone could have dreamed. His agents had tackled the impossible and come out on top time after time. His anger with the US government and the CIA in particular had not abated but only motivated him to establish a significant presence around the world. Funding from oil companies had planted his agents in Iraq long before the US invasion toppled Saddam Hussein. His men and women roamed the mountains of Afghanistan and brought back the kind of information that infuriated politicians who didn't want such things strewn across their local newspapers. He had foreseen the end of the Mubarak era long before anyone else expected it. Eric stayed on top of the action, and that made him, and those who paid him, happy.

Eric walked thoughtfully across his large estate in the mountains not far from Denver, Colorado. The warm summer breeze picked up, and a vulture circled overhead. The pines swayed in the wind, and across the valley he could see a mountain still splotched with patches of snow. A strong scent of pitch dripping from one of the trees filled his nose with the alluring aroma of summer. The beauty of the high country rejuvenated Eric and gave his mind freedom to soar.

The thick bed of pine needles crunched beneath his steps. Small finches fluttered among the tree branches, but Eric's thoughts turned back to harsh reality. The time had come to see if his agency could shake things up. A blitz media campaign detailing the evidence that the State Department had sequestered would expose how serious the drug situation had become in Afghanistan.

Through the trees, Eric could see the sprawling house built to look like a typical mountain home but constructed to hide the large underground complex beneath. Electronic equipment as well as a superb staff gave him instant contact with agents stationed all over the world. Every item ranging from the stock market to world news flashed across monitors. With sensors and security devices positioned around his estate, Eric felt secure. Even the US government would find it hard to penetrate his defenses.

Eric had chosen the name for the agency because it implied a mystery, a difficult problem to solve, and that was exactly what Eric and George Powers had built, an enigma, a puzzle within a riddle. Each agent and employee had proven to be a trusted friend many times over. The staff's commitment to the values of God and country made them sound like Boy Scouts, but in fact they were skilled agents of deception when the need presented itself. Their organization had remained impenetrable.

"Eric!" George Powers shouted from the veranda of Eric's sprawling home. "Up here! Need to talk to you right now."

"Coming." Eric picked up the pace. After crossing the

meadow between the trees and the house, he hurried up the wooden steps onto the veranda. Eric sat down at the ceramic-topped table. A pleasant breeze and warm sunlight drifted across the deck. "What's up?"

George stretched his long legs under the table. As usual, his flattop haircut imparted a college-boy appearance, but the wrinkles in his face betrayed the fact that he had left that world behind decades ago. His large eyes magnified by thick glasses widened further.

"We've got a problem, Eric." George seldom spoke in that tone of voice. Obviously, something had slipped through the cracks.

"Let me guess. Certain politicians are upset because we got that *New York Times* reporter Gordon Smith freed from Pakistan when the CIA didn't even know where he was. Instead of a thank-you, the big boys like to huff and puff that the time has come to even the score with us."

"I'm afraid this is much more serious." George crossed his arms over his chest and looked over the valley at the distant mountains.

"Is this a guessing game or what?"

"The CIA's coming after you. All that stink about the reporter threw a final log on the fire. Of course, your old friend Rowell Roach's been gone for some time, but he left a memo that put your name at the top of the troublemakers list. They've finally come up with an angle on how to sink your boat."

Eric took a deep breath. "Well, what's it going to be this go-round?"

"Unauthorized intelligence gathering."

"You're kidding."

"Afraid not. It's a little-known no-no, but it's on the books. The word that I'm picking up is that they have you coming and going on this. Certainly, our springing Gordon Smith out of Pakistan fills the bill. They're talking about putting you behind bars this time."

Eric laughed. "Worst-case scenario, I'll just trot down to Mexico and disappear for a while. I'm not worried."

George suddenly slammed his fist on the small table. "You don't get it! Listen to me. They mean business, Eric. You've always had this cocky sense of confidence like you're some kind of invincible Superman that can leap over government buildings with a single bound. You're not Superman, and I'm telling you that they are drawing up the papers to come after you right now."

Eric blinked several times.

"You can't win in court. You've already spread the Gordon Smith story all over the countryside. Moreover, the president himself is currently worried that you'll spill the beans on the regime in Afghanistan. The president wants you stopped."

Eric took a deep breath. "You're implying that they'll come after Conundrum and all of our employees?"

"Yes, but they want to put *you* out of business. This is personal."

"Is there an escape valve anywhere? Do we have any wiggle room?"

"I don't think so. Everyone up there on the Hill knows that your work is impeccable and that we seldom fail. Even if they hate your guts, they give you credit for being effective. Nevertheless, those folks want you gone."

"How much time do we have?" Eric asked.

"I don't have specifics, but I don't think they'll wait."

Eric looked out over the snowcapped mountains. A vulture still circled over the valley.

For the first time in years, he felt apprehension surge through his body. His adversaries had found a crack in the wall and were closing in. His days in the spying business could be numbered. The vultures were descending.

4

Long after George had gone back into the house, Eric sat on the veranda, staring into the pine forest and thinking about their conversation. He had never been a man to run. He hit problems head-on. He lived for challenges that everyone else avoided. During his sojourn in Egypt, he became well acquainted with the jihadists who believed that governments must be toppled through armed revolution. Out of the cataclysm would arise an Islamist society and finally a new nation run by Islamic sharia law. Eric had confronted those terrorists without reservation. But this new battle left him confounded.

He had always been straightforward, honest, and responsive to the point of getting himself in trouble. That's how it all began. He had done what the CIA told him to do, and that got him in hot water. The problem had been the agency's failure to stand behind their word, and that caused him to start his crusade to tell the truth regardless of where the chips fell. Rowell Roach had been part of the problem and would no doubt rejoice in Eric's current dilemma.

That afternoon in 1991 still burned in Eric's mind. Probably, he should have seen it coming. Every time he thought about the confrontation, his stomach churned. The entire mess had been a bitter pill, but it changed his life. The Conundrum had been born out of that conversation with Roach.

He had never liked or trusted Rowell Roach, the CIA's director of oversight, but Roach had responsibility for Eric's work.

Roach had stormed into the conference room like a bull. Roach intimidated most people; he lived by the adage "smash 'em in the nose before they know a fight's coming." Eric simply ducked; he would never back down.

Eric Stone was not easy to blindside. At the top of his class at Yale, he had been recruited by the CIA two months before graduation. His major in business administration contrasted with a minor in art and painting, but Eric had always been a strange combination of dreamer and pragmatist. He had a practical side, a head for clear thinking that at times could turn into hardheadedness. Faced with a difficult issue, the dreamer turned into an unsentimental straight shooter. The day after graduation, he started working as an agent in training. As a CIA agent, he had a reputation for catching all the details.

That day was no exception. Eric had known he was about to be canned.

Roach pulled a pack of cigarettes from his pocket and flipped one out. Through the office grapevine, Eric had learned that the director had emphysema. Eventually, the man would be forced to resign, and not long after, the disease would kill him.

On his notepad, Eric sketched a curl of smoke ascending above the director's head.

"I thought we couldn't smoke in this building," Eric said. "I got a memo."

"I wrote the memo," Roach replied with a tight edge in his voice.

"So much for consistency."

Director Roach didn't blink, but dropped into the chair like the captain of a submarine with nuclear weapons aimed at Stone. The squint in his eyes suggested he was about to fire.

"I read the full report in this file," he barked. "You're history, Stone."

Eric stopped sketching.

His training had taught him not to be agitated by threats. A gun in the face had to be taken seriously, but a word slinger usually only blew smoke. Roach always started by trying to make his opponent flinch.

"The Congress of the United States of America has found you guilty of perjury," Roach said. "You didn't tell them the truth about the Iran-Contra affair. Their independent investigation turned up evidence that arms were sent to Iran."

Eric nodded. "No news there. The agency ordered me to lie. Remember? You sat in the corner, listening. I did as I was told. End of story."

Roach leaned forward. "There's nothing in your file to indicate that you were given such an order."

"Of course not. The communications were all verbal. And if such an order had been in that file, you'd have destroyed it by now."

Roach looked irritated. "Don't get smart."

Eric penciled a quick sweeping black line under the face.

"You also told me that the president of the United States

would pardon me if the matter got sticky. Sounds like we're walking through flypaper now. The reprieve's still on?"

"There's no record of that promise either," Roach growled. "I don't know what you're talking about."

"Let's put it this way." Eric pulled a pen from his inside coat pocket. "You're looking at the world's smallest voice-activated video device. When I hit the tip, the pen starts working. Since the first day I walked through these doors, I've been using this to make sure the record stays straight. You'd be surprised at how well this little device works. I believe I do have the recording of the pardon you promised in a bank safety-deposit box. The TV news anchors would be delighted to get ahold of this, don't you think?"

Roach cursed. "You're young, but you don't miss a trick, do you?"

"Not when I'm dealing with old buddies with bad memories." Eric took a deep breath, and his voice became hard. "Is the pardon coming or not?"

Roach leaned back in his chair and popped his knuckles. "Yeah, you'll get one, but you'll have to resign. We may be able to get around the perjury charge without sending you to prison, but only if you keep your mouth shut. Read me? Shut tight."

Eric smiled, allowing Roach his moment. On his notepad, he scribbled "gotcha."

"Congress is packed with politicians who are tired of picking up newspapers and reading that Eric Stone called them swindlers and thieves," Roach said. "They want to shut you down. Now, do we have your resignation or are you going to make me haul you out to the dumpster in a wheelbarrow?"

Eric slowly reached in his inside coat pocket and pulled out an envelope. "Let me tell you the terms of our agreement."

Roach snorted, slowly shaking his head. "You still don't understand how it works, do you?"

Ignoring him, Eric laid his resignation letter on the table. "No problem with turning in my badge. But if I set one foot inside a prison cell, your voice and the entire story goes to CNN, FOX, ABC, NBC, CBS, and whoever else would like to broadcast it. You and the rest of this self-serving agency will be plastered on every newspaper in the world. Even Al Jazeera will get a shot at telling your miserable story to the Middle East." He shoved the envelope across the table. "I suggest you get to work on that pardon the minute I walk out the door or start planning for your reputation being worth about as much as Lee Harvey Oswald's."

Roach didn't reply, but his face turned a deep crimson.

Eric stood up. "See you around, Rowell. By the way, you might want to learn to walk slower and smoke less—you might live longer."

5

Eric Stone watched the four agents that made up his executive group take their seats in the conference room. He knew word was already out that they were in trouble. "George has information for us," he said with hardness in his voice. The room quieted. "Pay careful attention. We have decisions to make."

Eric's inner circle was a formidable lot. Each one had skills in unusual specialties that made them masters in the world of espionage. His top agents had gotten there by demonstrating that they kept their cool when situations turned ugly.

With the team gathered around a large mahogany table, Eric listened carefully to George detailing the warning he had given Eric earlier in the day. TV screens lined the walls. Each person had a laptop. An emergency red telephone sat in the middle of the table where any one of the five could answer it. The entire underground conference room had been sealed and soundproofed for absolute security.

George described how he had discovered the pending strike on their organization. The details painted an even bleaker picture of the government's attack than he had told Eric.

Through his complex computer connections with the government's surveillance systems, George had discovered the facts. A federal legal assault was imminent, and George's message was clear. In addition to an indictment, Eric might be arrested. The inner circle would be targets as well. The government had the Conundrum in their crosshairs.

Eric knew Sarah Fleming understood the problem well. Sarah had been a lawyer and an accountant with the FBI. A highly competitive person, Sarah played the world of numbers with amazing skill. She could make complex calculations dance. She also carried a one-pound Walther PPK-L pistol designed with concealability in mind. Her marksmanship was as exceptional as her math.

And Sarah had beauty to match the brains. With long flowing blonde hair and a model's face, she could pass for a cover girl modeling high-style clothes. Tall and slender, she looked delicate, but she was anything but. The truth was, she could break down a door.

Sarah's leather top with Indian-style fringe had been cut nearly to her navel. White lace around the top did the cover-up job and framed a squash-blossom silver necklace. Her large belt buckle framed a steer's head, finishing off the appearance of a Hollywood starlet. Her avant-garde appearance pushed the envelope, but then again, no one who saw her would think she was a spy. Eric watched Sarah sit there with a dreamy look in her eyes that suggested she was thinking about lounging on a beach in the Caribbean. Men had paid a high price for that illusion.

Sarah raised her hand. "George, is there any possibility that your time line could be off?"

George shook his head. "No, no chance."

To Eric's right, Jack Javidi scribbled on a small notepad. Always a prodigious note taker, Jack worked overtime to make sure he got things right. Emigrating from Iran over twenty years ago, Jack knew the inside story of the Middle East. His insights had been particularly valuable when the Conundrum started working in Iraq. Jack could cruise in and out of any of those countries, no questions asked. His handsome face and pleasant manner always attracted the women, but he kept such a low social profile that no one suspected he worked for a spy agency. While he bitterly despised the current Iranian regime, Jack respected the chaos they could create. He knew Iran kept racing toward building nuclear weapons that could blow the surrounding countries apart. While the Iranians hated Israel, Jack maintained they would be equally focused on toppling the king of Saudi Arabia, an idea that no one in Congress wanted to acknowledge publicly because the implications remained far too confounding.

When tension started boiling in Syria, Jack had wriggled his way into Baghdad and traveled down to the city of Latakia. After meeting with the local head of the National Association for Human Rights, Jack recognized the signs of unrest and building discontent. He watched discontent turn into explosive demonstrations. He was among the first to suggest that the town of Aleppo had been hit by chemical gas. Exiting the country before the Syrian army started trying to close the borders, Jack returned to the United States with the information that President Bari's regime had started killing citizens. Bari's credibility vanished, taking with it the United States's efforts at forming a new relationship with Syria.

"You're saying the CIA would come after each of us?" Jack pointed at his own chest.

"Right," George answered. "We must be prepared to shut down our operation immediately. How we do it and where we go is the pressing issue. I'm not talking about weeks. I'm suggesting hours, days at most."

"Do you mean that we might have to abandon this location?" Dan Morgan asked.

"Definitely," George said.

Eric had first met Dan when they both worked for the CIA. Dan's physical strength had been the stuff of legend. Time had not diminished his muscular body. At 250 pounds, he left the impression that challenging him would be painful. Eric thought of him as their enforcer. Dan looked like a mountain until he opened his mouth—he had the voice of a twelve-year-old boy. Eric trusted him with his life, many times.

"I yanked their political chains one time too many," Eric interjected. "We started the Conundrum with the intention of exposing government ineptitude, agency and congressional manipulations, and phony power plays. We won that war, but now the politicos are coming for us. Our options are limited. Of course, we can simply shut down the system and disappear."

"On the other hand, we could start over," Sarah said. "Get another name and keep right on working."

"Sure," George said. "But they want Eric. As best I can tell, they don't have any clear idea of how big our operation is. Each of you is vulnerable, but Eric's their main target. He's the guy they want to drop into the garbage disposal."

Dan shook his head. "These hypocrites think they can defeat us by legal maneuver. I suggest we outflank them."

"Thanks, Dan, but we're all shooting in the dark right now," Eric said. "Seems to me we ought to give ourselves twenty-four hours to digest the problem. We have people working in the field, and we've got to consider what's best for everyone. Let's sleep on the problem and see where we are when the sun comes up."

"Good idea," Jack said. "For one, I need more time."

"We can meet at the same time tomorrow," Eric said. "Let's come prepared to make decisions. It seems to me that—"

The telephone in the center of the table rang.

Eric looked at George. "Who could that be?"

"Don't know. Only a dozen of us have that number, and most of us are in this room."

The phone kept ringing.

"Answer it, George."

George picked up the phone. "Yes?" He paused. "I see. A meeting is *that* important?" After a few moments, he again said, "I see." Finally, he hung up the telephone.

"Well?" Eric asked.

"A woman says that you must meet her tomorrow at 11:30 at McGraw's Restaurant in Arvada."

"And who is *she*?" Eric asked.

"She said her name is Simone. Simone Koole."

6

Eric Stone and George Powers watched as the other agents filed out, but Eric's attention remained locked on the red telephone. Eric had picked it up at an estate sale because the color and style reminded him of the emergency phone that the White House had once used to contact the Kremlin before one side or the other blew up the world. Red had given the room a touch of color that reflected the urgency of the problems they faced. But seldom did anyone call.

"George, you've been around the world of espionage for twenty years. Ever hear of Simone Koole?"

"Rings no bells with me."

"How could she have gotten this phone number?"

George shook his head. "Beats me."

"The fact she did sets off fifty alarms in my head," Eric said. "I'd better show up at that restaurant."

"Yeah, that's the understatement of the day."

Long after George left the room Eric continued to think about the telephone call. Spying had always been a business of surprises. The point was to get the information first and startle the adversary. The Conundrum was supposed to be the ones handing out the big jolts, not the other way around. How could anyone from the outside get their hidden telephone number?

He would have to meet this woman. No question about it. As he pondered the issue, another unexpected situation returned to his mind. Back when the Conundrum was first coming into being, he had met George in the two-hundred-year-old Red Lion Pub in Washington. The quaint old colonial establishment had always been a good place for a confidential conversation. Eric remembered the unexpected announcement he had dropped on George. The entire scene once again returned with remarkable clarity.

Eric walked in and spotted George sitting in the back. On his way over to George's table, Eric glanced in a long mirror on a side wall and saw that he looked frazzled. His eyes had their usual intensity, but the dark blue had lost its sparkle. His black hair hung over his forehead in an uncharacteristic droop. His angular jaw usually looked straight off a recruiting poster for the Marines, but today he looked like he'd just walked off the battlefield.

One of the waitresses in a colonial costume with a neckline drifting toward the Mason-Dixon line walked by carrying a tray loaded with drinks. George waved from the booth. His Baltimore Ravens jacket didn't cover his fondness for Tootsie Rolls and cheeseburgers, but it gave him a just-an-average-guy appearance. His thick glasses made his eyes look like an owl searching for prey.

In the eighties, George had developed the ability to handle

what was then mind-boggling technology. For a short while, he had worked with the CIA, learning their system. His computer network had connections that even the connections didn't know about, so he'd heard what happened to Eric.

"Well, just look at us!" George began. "Two former CIA agents, one just cut loose from the payroll for the good of the country and the protection of his supervisor's job."

"So, you already know?"

"I saw it coming when they talked you into lying to Congress. They needed a fall guy, and you won the nomination."

"Ha-ha. And you gave up your career in espionage. You're a real Carnac the Magnificent."

"I'm just a humble security analyst who'll work for anybody who'll pay me a nickel."

"Maybe I can help you make some pocket change."

"Yeah, right. What do you want me to do? Climb inside Rowell Roach's computer and see if we can catch him fooling around with his secretary?" He leaned back, pushing his thick glasses further up his nose. "By the way, I don't think Roach is into hanky-panky at the office."

"Whether you know it for a fact or just made a good guess, I did get busted today. They fired me for congressional perjury and suggested that I might go to jail before this mess is over. If I keep my mouth shut, I might get a presidential pardon. You get the picture?"

"It's called 'hung out to dry.'"

"Well, I'm not turning into their wet laundry, no matter what Roach says, and I do not intend to take this problem lying down."

"You planning on declaring war on the CIA?"

"Something like that."

George laughed. "You want me to copilot a little 'bombs away' time over Langley, Virginia?"

"You think I'm kidding?" Eric leaned forward, popping his knuckles. The waitress walked up and asked if they wanted to order. They shook their heads, and she strolled away.

"What are you talking about?"

"I'm going to start my own spy agency."

George stared at him. "You mean like a detective firm?"

"No, I mean like the CIA."

"You gone nuts?"

"I'm serious. One of the reasons I got fired was that people in Congress didn't like the pressure I put on them. They're not ready to hear the truth. It gets in the way of the games they play."

"Look, Eric, I've done business with some big-time bad guys from around the world. That's small potatoes compared to what you're suggesting."

"That's why I want to hire you. You know the ropes. How things bounce. When to duck. And you can make a computer say the Pledge of Allegiance."

George took a deep breath. "Why don't you try selling insurance? Forget the wrestling match with Uncle Sam."

"I know what's ahead for this country," Eric said, brushing George's comments aside. "We're heading for big trouble in the Middle East. Nutcases like Saddam Hussein aren't going away. We got a jihad mentality blowing across the Middle East. I'm not going to sit it out and allow the Rowell Roaches and all the other little roaches run the country's intelligence agency like it's their personal playground. I'm going to assemble a team of spies and we're going after the truth regardless."

"Well, good luck and let me know where to send the money for your bail. No, wait. They won't arrest you. They'll kill you. Hey, if you die, can I have your baseball card collection?" He shook his head. "Count me out. I'd rather sit in my nice quiet office and read about you in the newspapers."

"C'mon, George. America needs your talents and resources more today than it ever has. You can play the clown, but in your heart, you know you're as frustrated as I am. This is your chance. You want the best for this nation as much as I do."

George squirmed. "Man, you're talking big time here. We could have the entire federal system breathing down our necks."

"Not if they don't know where to find us. And I'm the master at disappearing and coming up for air only when I'm ready. I'm going to give the CIA and those congressional fat cats real old-fashioned fits. And I need your help."

George ran his hands nervously through his hair. "I can't believe you'd take on the entire CIA. How are you going to fund this little private army of yours?"

"I've got a stack of names of people who'd be more than glad to fund me if I gave back solid information and security. Money isn't an issue."

"You really think you can pull this off?" George said.

Eric grinned. "Watch and see. Round one's about to begin."

The memory faded, and Eric realized he was once again staring at the red telephone and the empty chairs around the room. He had done what he set out to do back in 1991. Now George needed to get him out of hot water one more time. Only he couldn't see any way to do it.

7

The sprawling mall stood on the edge of Denver's suburb of Arvada not far from the town of Golden. Eric turned into Colorado Mills Shopping Center and drove cautiously down the back side. One thought kept rumbling around in his mind. How could anyone have acquired the Conundrum's secret phone number? No one on the inside would have leaked it. Could some client have stumbled onto the number and passed it on? Not possible. And who was Simone Koole? George said she had an accent that he couldn't place. He had found nothing on the internet. What could this woman be after?

Eric pulled into McGraw's nearly empty parking lot. Of course, 11:15 in the morning was on the early side. Shutting his car door, he glanced around the parking lot. Nothing looked unusual. Dan Morgan had already cased the area and the restaurant.

The restaurant had a dark-brown wooden exterior that suited the mountain setting well. The interior walls were lined with pictures of fishermen catching everything from huge salmon to hordes of codfish. The atmosphere felt cozy enough, but that would provide a disarming setting if someone wanted to stage a hit. McGraw's Restaurant fit the relaxed mold, and that was why it could be a natural setup to catch him off guard. Eric nudged his chest to make sure his shoulder holster kept his Glock 9mm pistol in place.

A waiter seated him in a booth near the back of a side dining room. A waitress wearing a blue head scarf looked busy pouring water. No one else sat in his section. Despite Dan's earlier inspection, this smelled like a trap. Casually, he pushed the tip of his pen, activating the video device. He was ready.

If no one showed in ten minutes, he was out of there. Maybe the government snoops had set up this meeting to lure him into an easy setting where they could grab him. Drag him out the back door. Drug him. Whatever. Eric didn't like any of it.

He looked around the restaurant again. Many times he had eaten at this fish house. Eric had never married, so he dined by himself much of the time. Along the way, there'd been serious romances, and once he'd nearly walked down the aisle. But Eric believed that no woman should have to live with a man who could, on any day of the week, get a bullet in his head. In the middle of the night, a call could send him flying halfway around the world. On more than one occasion, he'd landed in some remote hospital in the backwaters of a third world country. Marriage didn't fit in his plans.

He glanced at his watch and checked his voice-activated pen. Five minutes had passed. Two more minutes and that was it. Forget the other three.

The waitress set a glass of water on the table. "Are you ready to order?" she said.

He studied the woman for a moment. Black hair covered with a blue scarf. Dark complexion. No makeup, but not ordinary. Attractive. Black hair framing a narrow face with high cheek bones. Regular working appearance. Nothing unusual there.

"I need another minute," Eric mumbled out of habit.

Pulling off her head scarf, the woman abruptly sat down across from him and laid the dark blue silk on the table. She shook her head, and long black hair fell over her shoulders. Her eyebrows arched in a gentle curve while her gaze fastened on him like magnets grabbing iron. "Good morning, Mr. Stone. I hope you are ready." She extended her hand. "Simone Koole."

Eric reached out and shook her hand mechanically. Her grip was cool, strong, but feminine at the same time. For a moment, he almost felt light-headed.

"H-how'd you get my phone number?"

"That's the business I am in," Ms. Koole said with a slight accent.

"Well, you're certainly not a local."

Ms. Koole merely smiled.

"You with any organization I know?"

She raised an eyebrow. "Definitely."

Eric leaned back in his seat. The woman was toying with him. "You called the meeting, Ms. Koole. Why don't you tell me what it's about."

"If you play your cards right, I can help you out of the hole you've dug for yourself with the CIA."

"What hole?" Eric hoped he sounded innocent.

"The one that looks like a grave."

George had been able to pick up on the planned shutdown of Eric's organization because of his unusual computer connections with government offices. To his knowledge, no one in the CIA knew George was on to the story yet. Simone Koole must be from the inside of the inside of the Feds.

"A grave?"

"Let's quit feeling each other out," Ms. Koole said. "We both know that your government is getting ready to shut you down."

She had said "*your* government." The slip implied Simone Koole was from a foreign service. Maybe the phrase was a mistake on her part; maybe not. But it was a clue.

"How does a foreign agent pick up such secrets from the inner circles of the American intelligence establishment?"

"We're quite good at what we do," she said. "You're still trying to figure out who I am, so let me help you. I'm with Mossad."

Eric stared her down. "All right, Ms. Koole, you seem to be in charge of this conversation. You tapped into a highly secret telephone line, and you've also tapped into highly classified information. I have no idea where our discussion is going. So, why don't you tell me?"

"Please call me Simone. I need your help on a project, and I doubt if Conundrum would get involved in what I am proposing under ordinary circumstances. However, if you cooperate with me, I can make sure your current problem disappears. If you don't, then I would suggest you start packing."

"I'm sure you won't tell me, but I have to ask. How did you slice into our telephone line?"

"No comment." Simone smiled. "Any more questions?"

"How did you get inside the CIA?"

The woman continued to smile. "Classified as well."

"We're both in the intelligence game and you want my help, but you won't throw out any more info?" Eric frowned. "Little on the unfair side, isn't it?"

"Definitely. But when did we start playing fair?" Simone kept smiling, but there was an edge of steel in her voice that told him she knew she had him and was only waiting for him to admit it. "The bottom line is if you and your people cooperate with me, your current troubles are over. Refuse and you're on your own. The matter is that simple."

No point in trying to make an end run. Simone Koole was driving the bus, and the best he could do was hang on.

A waitress walked up. "Sorry. I didn't see anyone back here. May I bring you anything to drink? Coffee? Tea?"

"Coffee's fine," Simone said.

"Hot tea, please." Eric took a deep breath. "I suppose we won't be ordering for a while."

The waitress walked away.

"I need to talk this offer over with my staff," Eric said. Simone didn't blink or smile. She might know all about George or Sarah, even have Jack's home phone; she might know nothing. Maybe she'd make another slip and he'd learn more. Eric waited for her response.

"Our time is limited. I can only give you forty-eight hours to respond. I will leave a cell phone number with you. When you call, you will say either 'yes' or 'no' and I'll go from there. That's it."

"Look, Simone, my people need to know what you want us to work on. We're both in a confidential business, after all."

Simone merely stared at him for a long second before repeating. "Yes or no. That's all I need to hear."

The waitress set two cups on the table. "Would you like to order something to eat?"

"Not at the moment," Simone said and picked up her cup.

Eric breathed out frustration. "You want me to commit my people and my resources without knowing what the job is, where it is, or how dangerous it might be? Right?"

"You've got it." Simone reached for her scarf.

"We need more details. Who are we after?"

"We will take it one step at a time. I will tell you on a piece-by-piece basis where we're going. That's all you'll get." Simone sipped her coffee.

"Let me get this straight. My team does something for you and all my troubles with the government vanish?"

"Exactly."

"And you can guarantee that?"

"Absolutely."

"We've never done it this way before," Eric said.

"You've never been in this much trouble before," Simone said.

Telling him nothing left her completely in charge. Simone Koole definitely intended to run the show.

"We get paid?"

"Of course," Simone said. "The usual rate. Expenses. A healthy stipend."

Eric nodded. "And how do we know you're on the up-and-up?"

"If you want verification of my authenticity, call the Mossad offices in Tel Aviv. Normally they'd hang up on you. Tell them who you are and ask about me. You'll get an answer."

"I suppose you know that you have me against a wall," Eric said. "My people don't like flying blind."

"My people have always lived with unpredictable circumstances," Simone said. "Moses had to push Pharaoh to the brink before the Egyptian ruler responded. Jews have become accustomed to facing impossible odds."

Eric shook his head. "I understand that Mossad's motto comes straight out of the Bible."

"'Where there is no guidance, a people fails; but in an abundance of counselors there is safety.'" Simone smiled. "From Proverbs."

"Your people seem to take the Bible seriously," Eric said. "You think God is on your side?"

"It's more important for us to be on God's side."

Eric laughed. "Most intelligence agents don't give a moment's reflection on religious stuff."

"I suppose it would be difficult for you to imagine." Simone's voice softened and became more reflective. "Of course, many Jews don't practice their religion and see themselves as only an ethnic entity. Such is true in *Eretz-Israel*. However, we are alive today only because *HaShem* has guided us through difficult times. We exist because *Adonai* exists."

"So, you think God works with you and the Jewish people?"

"You misplaced the emphasis again. The issue is *our* working with *him*."

"Fascinating." Eric rubbed his chin. "Haven't thought about this stuff since I was a boy in Sunday school."

"My life rests in the hands of the God of Abraham, Isaac, and Jacob, and I passionately serve only him." Simone leaned over the table. "And what is your god, Eric?"

Eric raised his eyebrows in surprise. "In my entire career in espionage, no one has ever asked me that. I suppose my answer would be that I believe in the righteous purposes of the United States of America. I serve that singular destiny as relentlessly as you serve your God."

Simone nodded. "Now that we have the religious issues out of the way, we can return to the matter at hand." She stood up, picked up the scarf she had been wearing. "I will expect to hear from you in forty-eight hours." She pushed a card across the table with numbers scribbled on the back. "Give me a call."

Simone walked out nonchalantly. Usually in complete control, today Eric felt in free fall. Never had another agent left him so disoriented. He felt sure the next forty-eight hours would prove equally disconcerting.

The waitress appeared with a pencil and pad in hand. "What will you have?"

Eric looked at his full teacup for a long moment. "You know . . . I think I've lost my appetite."

8

Silence settled over the group seated around the long table in the underground chambers of Eric's estate and offices. Eric tapped on his voice-activated video pen now operating over loudspeakers on the walls. Simone Koole's image flashed across the overhead screens. The Conundrum's executives watched her sitting across from Eric and transforming herself from café servant to spy.

"Good morning, Mr. Stone." The video playback captured every detail. *"I hope you are ready. Simone Koole."*

Each of the four top advisers leaned forward.

"I swear that woman appeared out of nowhere," Dan said. "I cased McGraw's inside and out."

"Don't beat yourself up too much," Eric said. "I have a feeling that woman can walk through walls."

The executive committee listened intently to his conversation with Koole. After the Mossad agent walked out, Eric turned the recording off, and the TV screens went blank.

"I can't believe it," Jack said.

"You better," Sarah replied. Her striking bright yellow top covered with the imprint of lemons and leaves had sleeves hanging down at least a foot from her arms with bright gold amulets covering her wrists. "The woman obviously had access to inside information that we had no idea even existed until yesterday." Sarah's flowing blonde hair swung when she shook her head vigorously. "We shouldn't underestimate her capabilities."

George's big eyes became even more intense. "She could be a plant to lure us into a trap. Our CIA pals may know more than we think they do."

"But what if she's the real thing?" Dan pressed. "She's got to know we'll check her out. I believe our first step is to make sure she really is an agent with Mossad."

"Dan's right," Eric said. "If she's Mossad, at least we know we're not being conned."

George glanced at his watch. "It would be morning in Tel Aviv. Mossad's office should be open for business."

Sarah pointed at the phone in the center of the conference table. "We once thought this connection was secure. Simone Koole destroyed that idea, but we could still use the line to call overseas."

"I keep a listing of intelligence agencies around the world. Need 'em on occasion." George pushed a small book across the table toward Eric. "We can find out quickly enough."

Eric thumbed through the book and then began tapping in the numbers. Quiet fell over the room. After a few moments, the long buzzing resounded. The phone rang only twice.

"*Boker tov*," a woman's voice said.

"I'm calling from America," Eric said. "Do you speak English?"

"Yes." A slight accent.

"I'm calling about agent Simone Koole. Can you give me someone to verify her employment?"

"Just a moment," the woman said. The telephone went on hold.

A man's voice came on the line. "Hallo."

"My name is Eric Stone. I'm from the United States."

"We have been expecting your call," the man said in a heavy accent. "I am Dar Dagan. You have called to verify Simone Koole's relationship with our organization. I believe you go by the name the Conundrum."

"That's correct."

"I can assure you, Ms. Koole is one of our finest employees, and what she told you is correct. You will find her to be a capable person. Is there more you need to know?"

"Yes, I want to know where this mission is going. What's the nature of the assignment?"

"In due time you will know. Simone will tell you as she sees fit. Thank you for calling." The telephone went dead.

Eric slumped back in his chair. "She's for real. A Mossad agent."

George pushed his glasses up his nose. "Maybe we're actually on our way out of this mess."

"Everybody ready to proceed on this venture?" Eric asked. Every hand went up.

"Okay. I'll call this mystery woman and tell her that we're on. Let's get back to work."

The agents left the room, but Eric sat in his chair staring at the red telephone in the center of the table.

9

The Boeing 757 slowly circled over Boston and then descended to the runway. The airplane bounced a couple of times before turning toward the terminal. Coming off the airplane, Simone Koole blended into the crowd. Wearing jeans and an old blue jersey pullover with her black hair pulled back in a ponytail, she looked like a college student on her way home. Simone sauntered down the long corridor at a leisurely pace. Near the fifth gate, a café with small tables lined the large windows looking over the tarmac. A forlorn-looking man sat in the shadows, nursing a cup of coffee and chewing on a cigar. His bald head reflected light from the windows behind him. When she approached the table, the man did not stand up or look at her. For a moment she stood motionless.

"*Boker tov*," she said.

He patted the tabletop gently and she sat down.

"We should speak Hebrew, Benny," Simone said. "Don't want to be overheard."

Benny Gantz nodded his agreement. "They contacted Tel Aviv. Dagan himself took their call."

"They're buying the story?"

"Looks like it. Stone should call within a few hours. It appears that our plan is running full tilt."

"Excellent," Simone said. "Any other information?"

"A story you'll like," he said in hushed tones. "Last night our boys discovered a ship flying a Liberian flag sailing about two hundred miles off Israel. Commandos from the navy's Flotilla 10 came roaring in under darkness and boarded the vessel."

"You mean the ship we spotted being loaded at a Syrian port?"

"Exactly. After they left Syria, the cargo carrier went to southern Turkey before departing from the Port of Mersin. We knew the containers being put on board were suspicious. Our agents observed armed troops standing around while the shipments were hoisted aboard. You don't load lentils and cotton while the local warriors have their Vektor R4s aimed at everyone in sight. We knew they had to be shipping tools for evil. Two Iranian warships docked there earlier in the year."

"What happened?"

"The ship's captain complied with our commandos' demands. In short order, navy personnel found crates marked commerce that had been fitted with heavy padlocks. And sure enough, inside were crates of mortar shells as well as the jackpot: C-704 anti-ship missiles."

"Ah!" Simone beamed. "Six C-704s from China could have wrecked the balance of power in the region. Our people struck a major blow against Iran and their Hamas buddies. Iran is boxed in."

"Thought you'd like that little report."

"It fills my heart with joy. I'm sure the people at the Office are equally pleased."

"Even the Dragon quit breathing fire."

"Who was directing their operation?" Simone asked.

"Looks like a General Sayyid al-Banna who currently oversees Iran's arms efforts. He once headed the Iranian Revolutionary Guard's Quds Force. The man's been sending weapons to Africa for some time. Not a nice guy."

"I'm sure he won't be happy explaining our little intervention to the mullahs. You are on your way back to Israel?"

"I have a ticket for tonight's flight. I will be waiting for your call after our friends in Denver respond. If all systems are go, I will receive your instructions for taking the next step."

"I will say that the chase is on. Of course, if there is some unexpected problem, then I will have to say more."

"When I arrive in Tel Aviv, I will go to the Office and talk with the dragon man."

Simone laughed. "Make sure he doesn't blow fire. He can singe your eyebrows off."

Leaning back in his chair, Benny rolled his eyes and grinned. "That's how I lost my hair." He winked.

"You have a weird sense of humor, Benny."

He looked at her with eyes that had shifted from jocular to sad. "My heart is always heavy, Simone. Too many have been killed. I've been responsible for too many deaths."

Simone studied Benny's face. His eyes had taken on a bottomless character that made him appear to be drifting into another world.

"I know," she said. "I know."

"Our job is hard. Too hard."

She squeezed his hand. "Someday we can all sit out in the fresh air by the Dead Sea and let the sun wash away our wounds. Now our job is to protect the people who already are resting out there in the gentle breeze. Buck up, Benny. We must keep on."

He nodded his bald head. "Let's have a nice glass of wine."

Simone leaned back in her chair. "Ever hear of Nadab and Abihu?"

Benny scratched his head. "Nadab and Abihu? What's that got to do with anything? Say, wait a minute. Didn't those guys run a delicatessen on Ben Yehuda Street several years ago?"

"Really, Benny! You can be a moron. Didn't you ever go to classes at the synagogue?"

He shrugged. "I grew up in a secular family. My father believed religion got the Jews in trouble so he didn't want to take a dose."

"Back to Nadab and Abihu. They weren't merchants in Jerusalem. You'll find them in the book of Leviticus. They were priests in the Temple who came to work half-loaded, and the Holy One, blessed be he, destroyed them for their arrogance in failing to pay attention."

"They got wiped out for drinking?" Benny frowned and leaned back.

"The book of Leviticus points out that *HaShem* forbade drinking while they were working in the Temple. When they were on duty, it was important to stay sober and keep their minds on business. Hear me? Pay attention lest you get your head blown off."

Benny shrugged. "I guess it's good that you take this stuff seriously."

"You'd better do the same if you want to keep your head on your shoulders."

10

Afternoon shadows fell over the hauntingly beautiful mountain scene. Pine trees dotted the hills, and a red hawk sailed in a large circle over the magnificent landscape. Eric turned away from the window back to George and Sarah sitting across the desk from him.

"We've got to find more information on this Simone Koole," Eric said.

Sarah nodded. "She won't be easy to track."

"That's why I want you to be the search engine, Sarah." Eric leaned over the desk. "At this point, a woman trailing the mystery woman makes more sense. You'd be less likely to be noticed. We need you to fly because time is of the essence."

"Mossad agents are tough customers." Her long sleeves dangled nervously beneath her silk top imprinted with brilliant red poppies. "Tell me everything you know."

"She's been in Denver but undoubtedly lives somewhere else," Eric said. "George, you can zero in on people with the name Simone Koole."

"Sure. There's probably only ten to fifty thousand of them hanging around this country." George shrugged cynically.

"She might not go by that name. How many you want me to run down?"

"Can you hack into the NSA?" Eric asked.

George rubbed his chin. "The CIA is after us, and now you want to make the NSA mad too?"

Sarah glared at George. "The National Security Administration just built their own secret city in San Antonio big enough to hold all the information in the world. Surely you can find a way to get in."

"Well, well, Sarah's suddenly found unlimited confidence in me."

"Sarah has a point, George. You can climb over their firewall."

"Well, the NSA does have a department called the Terrorist Identities Datamart Environment, or TIDE. In addition, the National Counterterrorism Center has names. I understand it's the mother of all watch lists. It's one more list I can check to get at all the names out there. Let me see what I can find."

"Sarah will need this information by morning. I'm dispatching her to chase down what we can find out about Simone Koole."

"I'll be here at six in the morning." Sarah stood up.

"You might wear something less flashy," George said.

❖❖❖

The blowing yellow sand swirled down the labyrinth of narrow alleyways winding across the Gaza Strip. Behind high walls topped with shards of broken glass, women in long burkas walked down the street alongside men wearing gray sweaters perpetually buttoned in even the hottest weather.

Sitting in battered sidewalk café chairs and puffing the sweet flavored smoke from a hookah, two men talked in hushed whispers.

"Our Hamas leaders have finally chosen you to go after this woman who has caused our people so much trouble," Ali al-Hazmi said.

Abd al-Rashid smiled. "I am honored. I have been to Yemen and Egypt, but I have never been to the United States. I look forward to this trip." The strong breeze scattered his black hair combed over the side of his face to cover the angry scar running from the side of his ear into his scalp.

"Your task will not be easy," al-Hazmi said. "However, explosives and weapons are waiting in America. You will be able to strike quickly and return."

"Do you think anyone has been tracking me?"

Al-Hazmi shook his head. "We have chosen you for this reason. We believe you can enter the country without notice. We are counting on your anonymity. Just keep your hair combed down over your ear."

"A woman should prove easy to kill."

"Don't misjudge her. She is quite capable of cutting your throat in hand-to-hand combat. What you must do must be done quickly, and best from a distance." Al-Hazmi squeezed al-Rashid's arm. "Do you understand me?"

"I am not afraid of a woman!"

"Listen to me carefully, Abd. We have not been sending our people across the ocean, but we are making an exception to avenge al-Mabhoub's death in the Arab Emirates hotel. You must not make a mistake or you will come home in a wooden box. This woman has been highly trained. If you underestimate her, you will be dispatched to the same place where al-Mabhoub now dwells."

Rashid leaned back and smiled. "I understand. Do not worry, my friend. I will assess the situation carefully."

"Do that." Al-Hazmi pushed an envelope across the table. "You will find your tickets and a passport with a new name as well as credit cards and American dollars. A list of addresses and various aliases she has used. Memorize them and then discard the list. A car is waiting to take you to Egypt. The driver will give you further instructions. You will fly from Cairo to Washington DC. Luggage has already been packed so there is no need to return to your house. When we finish talking, you will leave."

"So soon?"

"Yes. We cannot afford any hitches in our plans. Tell no one of your departure. While you are gone, we will pray for Allah's protection. Do you have any more questions?"

Rashid shook his head. "I am ready."

❖·❖·❖

The first light of day bathed Eric Stone's house in golden sunlight. Cool mountain night air invigorated Sarah as she pulled into the driveway. She entered the hidden basement area through a side door and flipped on the hall light, dispelling the darkness.

"Who's there?" George called out.

"Sarah."

"Oh. Well, I hope you appreciate I've been here all night working for you."

"I'm sure I've been in your every thought."

George snorted. "Not in the way that you'd like. Around 2:00 a.m., your face turned a little fuzzy."

"Okay, George. Did you find anything?"

"I know you doubt my abilities, but you'll be surprised."

"Really?"

"There must be a thousand Simone Kooles in the United States in whom we have absolutely no interest. More in Canada. However, I did climb over the firewall at the NSA's website. Guess what I found."

"Don't toy with me, George. I've got a long day ahead."

"In the back of their National Counterterrorism Center they have a listing of aliases. Seems a Susan Brown came from Israel recently with a passport that connected to their system. Good old Susan uses the name Alice Rhymer, May Nixon, and Joan Border as well. However the Center tells me the names all belong to one Jewish woman named Simone Koole. How's that grab you?"

"Well, for once you did something right, George. I'm amazed."

"Furthermore, Susan Brown lists a potential residence in Washington DC. No street names or numbers, though. All the phone numbers I came up with for you to check when you hit the ground are ready. Being in Washington gives you the ability to respond immediately to anything you find."

"So, I'm off to DC?"

"Yep. You'll need to be hitting the pavement in order to find this Simone Koole. For the sake of time, you can run these names when you get there. If you hurry into Denver, you can catch the flight that I've already booked for you."

"A little presumptuous, but okay."

He shoved a packet across the table. "If you run into trouble, here's a source of final recourse. I have an old friend with expertise in running down people impossible to find. If all else fails, call him. The guy's British and can be difficult. Ignore the nonsense and he'll come through. We always called him "the Sniffer." His name, information, and number are in the packet. I've already lined up the stops for you. How can you ever deny my abilities now?"

"Just because you did something right *once* doesn't mean it makes up for a mountain of past and future mistakes." Sarah grinned and swung her long blonde hair around the back of her neck. "After all, I've survived terrible injustices at your hands."

George started laughing. "If we only had violins playing in the background. Okay, queen of vaudeville, keep us dancing. You've got a load of material that should send you on your way with a smile."

11

Afternoon sunlight streamed through the large windows overlooking the airplanes sitting on the tarmac of Reagan National Airport. Sarah walked in, scanning the terminal. Nothing looked unusual. A second survey revealed nothing more than a typical Washington airport scene. The slight smell of coffee and a stronger scent of hot pizza floated through the air.

She glanced at her reflection in the large windows. The heavy-knit blue sweater that hung below her hips was a bit understated for her usual taste. Against her tight black stretch pants, the color seemed bright enough. Maybe the black patent leather shoes with stiletto heels and the bright red leather gloves made too big a splash. She stuck the gloves in her purse.

A few international flights had been routed into terminal two, and one was arriving from Cairo. She walked to one of the few remaining banks of telephones and sat down. A cell phone could be traced, so she preferred the anonymity of the public phones. Pulling out the list of names she had received from George, Sarah began working the phone lines.

"Hello," a low voice said.

"I'm calling for Susan Brown."

"Well, you got her. What can I do for you?"

"Would you be Jewish?"

"No. Why would you ask that?" The woman sounded confused.

"Thank you. Sorry to have bothered."

Sarah figured it would be a long, long day. She started to dial the next number. Across the hall, passengers began filing out of the exit door under a blinking sign that read Cairo. Sarah always paid strict attention to her surroundings but particularly when they related to the Middle East. Businessmen and tourists slowly filed into the terminal. The passengers looked like the long overnight flight had given them plenty of wear. A little extra sleep wouldn't hurt any of them.

A young man walked off, carrying a small duffel bag. Stopping just inside the terminal, he looked awed at the sights around him. Sarah continued watching him. He rubbed his eyes and pushed his hair back out of his face. Only then did she notice the nasty red scar that ran up from his ear into his scalp. The man started walking toward the telephones. Sarah looked away lest she appeared to be staring—which she was.

Once again she dialed a number the operator had given her. "Susan Brown, please."

"Ma'am, Susan hasn't lived here in over a year."

"Thank you." Sarah hung up.

The sound of an accented voice carried over from the booth next to her. "Number for Susan Brown."

Sarah froze.

"Thank you," the man said.

She leaned her head into the metal partition.

"Looking for Susan Brown," the man said and waited. "Oh, I see. Good-bye."

A man got off an airplane from Cairo and wanted to contact an American named Susan Brown? Hardly a coincidence. The man with the scar would bear watching. She listened as he made several more phone calls, always asking for a Susan Brown. After six calls, he picked up the duffel bag and started walking.

Sarah immediately fell in behind him. Whoever this man might be, there had to be a connection with her own search. Dropping back twenty feet, she watched him as he walked through the airport. The man didn't appear to have any sense that he was being followed. Once they crossed through the security exit gate, he picked up the pace. Only then did he start looking behind him. On the second squint, Sarah sensed that he might have noticed her. She pulled back farther.

The man picked up his pace and darted around a corner. Sarah hurried to the wall's edge and peered around the corner. Almost running, he had made it through the exit. She doubled her pace, but he had already reached the curb. Sarah watched his taxi pull away.

She had bumped into the man from Cairo by coincidence, but there was nothing accidental in his intentions. Something was up, but she had no idea what it was—and he was gone.

12

By evening, Sarah's patience had worn thin. Her phone inquiries had gotten her nowhere. She kept thinking about the man from Cairo. Coincidence? Providence? Accident?

Her cell phone rang. "Hello."

"I didn't mean to wake you," George said.

"Ha-ha." Sarah's voice stayed flat. "What did you find on the airline's passenger list?"

"Nothing. I have no leads for you."

"Well, I've found none here either."

"Remember 'the Sniffer'? Try him for a lead."

Sarah drummed on the metal phone stand for a moment. "Well, I've got nothing to lose."

"Trust me, the Sniffer will do the trick."

"Okay. See ya." Sarah hung up and dialed the number George had given her earlier. "Hello. I'm looking for a man called the Sniffer."

"Yeah?" The man's voice sounded unusually high pitched over the phone. "And who's looking for the old Sniffer?"

"Name is Sarah Fleming. George Powers sent me."

"George? No foolin'!"

"That's the man."

"Well, Ms. Fleming, what can I do for you?"

"I'm looking for a woman using the alias Susan Brown who recently came in from Israel. Her real name is Simone Koole and she lives somewhere in the Washington DC area. Can you find her in thirty minutes?"

"You're talking to the old London bloodhound himself. But before we go any further, who you working for? I don't exactly walk about the streets handing out me cards, you know. If you're with the cops, you got the wrong number."

"George said you might be difficult at first. Let's put it this way. You're doing this for the Conundrum, and they'll be paying you. How's that?"

"Old George is still hanging out with Eric Stone, eh? Okay, you got a cell phone number?"

"I don't normally give out my cell phone number, but I'll make an exception if you come up with an answer in thirty minutes."

"Well, aren't you demanding? Truth is, I owe George one, so I'll do the job for him. How's that sound, Ms. Fleming?"

"Thirty minutes?"

The man laughed. "Yeah. If I can do it in thirty minutes, I figure it's worth at least a couple of grand. Okay? You got any phone numbers for the ol' Sniffer?"

"I've run my list down to the bottom. The problem is I can't get an answer at some of these numbers. I'll give the remainder to you. And the fee is accepted."

Sarah read off the phone numbers quickly. "This woman also uses the names May Nixon, Joan Border, and Alice Rhymer, if that helps."

"Every tidbit is worth checking. Sit tight, Fleming. The Sniffer will be back." The line went silent.

Time was pressing. She had hoped to call Eric with some specific information and needed to get on the street to find this woman. If this guy could produce anything in thirty minutes or even an hour, it was more than worth the price. Eric needed any insight she could come up with, but the telephone calls had gone south along with the man from Cairo. She began pacing.

Thirty minutes later almost to the second, the phone rang. Sarah grabbed it from her purse. "Yeah."

"Don't the ol' Sniffer deserve more than a one-word greeting?"

"We'll send flowers on your birthday," Sarah said.

"Well, that's more like it. I think I have what you're looking for."

Sarah took a deep breath. "Okay. Shoot."

"When you hang around town, you make acquaintances. I've got friends on the police force, agents in the CIA, buddies in the FBI. Just old pals hanging out everywhere with information. So, I called one of the boys down at a local precinct and told him who I was looking for. Under the table, he had me call the Intelligence Authorization Office and use a particular name, which I won't mention. A few of my persuasive words and they gave me an address. Can't tell you it's secure, but your Susan Brown originally landed there. That's a fact. You'll have to check it out."

"I'm ready."

The man rattled off an address and directions from the airport. Sarah scribbled as fast as possible.

"Well, it seems that the Sniffer did come through," Sarah said. "Remember to send your bill to the Conumdrum to the attention of Sarah Fleming."

"Hey, anytime you need a skip tracer, you know where I am."

"I appreciate your help."

"Good-bye." The phone clicked off.

◇-◇-◇

The rental car took her across the Potomac River, down Connecticut, and close to Rock Creek Park. The Sniffer's directions had been detailed and proved easy to follow. She passed a small neighborhood shopping center with a Grab N Go fast-food store and a couple of small-items shops nearby. Sarah knew she had to be close.

At the next corner, she turned left and slowed. Lane Street. The Sniffer had said it was a blue two-story house. Small. Secluded. Five houses down Sarah could see the sky color with black shutters on each side of the front windows.

"Jackpot!" she said out loud.

Sarah pulled to the curb. A woman was unloading groceries out of the back of an old Honda. Blonde hair. Older. Wrong age. Didn't look anything like Simone Koole.

"I'm sorry to bother you," Sarah said. "But I'm looking for a person that I thought lived at this location."

The woman eyed her suspiciously. "I don't know anyone in the neighborhood. Been here only a short time."

"Oh." Sarah nodded thoughtfully. "The person I'm looking for was named Susan Brown."

"We only moved in two days ago. But come to think of it,

I believe the last name of the previous tenant was Brown. I never met her, though. Sorry."

"You have no idea where she moved?"

"I mind my own business." The woman's words carried an accusation and the hint she had no more to say. Picking up a sack of groceries, she started toward the back door. After a few steps, she stopped. "Sorry that I can't help."

"Thank you." Sarah got back in the car.

She knew George had run the names down through every internet site. The truth couldn't be avoided. Simone Koole was nowhere to be found. Sarah had hit a dead end.

13

Eric watched several computers work simultaneously while George kept clicking in data and printing out responses. George studied each printout carefully but found nothing. Somewhere out there in cyberspace there had to be an answer, but they weren't finding it.

Eric glanced at his watch. "Sarah found nothing. George, we're running out of time. I've got to call Ms. Koole quickly or I'll miss her deadline. Found anything?"

George pulled off his thick glasses and rubbed his eyes. "Not about her, but here's the strange thing. My connections seem to have dried up."

"What do you mean?"

"I've tried every angle from the FBI to the Department of Justice. The CIA hasn't been making any comments either. No one is talking about us anywhere. It's like the stream of information simply stopped flowing."

"What do you make of it?"

George shook his head. "I don't know. Until yesterday, the lines were popping. Boom! Today they're silent."

Jack Javidi walked in. "I've been running my database on the Middle East and found a couple of trouble spots."

"What do you have?" Eric asked.

"I can't figure out why this woman wants us to help her. They've got Mossad people all over Syria. I can't see how we have any connections in Jordan they would value. Nothing adds up right. Koole could want us to help gather data on the violence in Lebanon. Lots of trouble there. But why us?"

Eric rubbed his chin. "Sure. Anything else?"

"Egypt. Maybe the Israelis want us to help figure out what's working below the social surface in Cairo. After all, the Muslim Brotherhood is always a genuine threat to Israel's security." Jack shrugged. "All shots in the dark, but they might be why this woman showed up on our doorstep."

"Thanks, Jack," Eric said. "George, keep checking."

Eric stepped out into the corridor and yelled, "Sarah! Sarah, can you come down to George's office right now?"

Sarah stepped out of her office. "Don't you guys ever use the phone?" Wrapped in a high-collar Burberry black-and-white tweed jacket with thick turned-up lapels that looked like London high society, Sarah strolled in wearing leather riding boots. "I just got back in town five minutes ago."

"Look at you," George grumbled. "Don't you ever dress like a normal person?"

"If you call yourself normal, I'll pass." Sarah smiled nonchalantly and pulled at a strand of her long blonde hair. "You wouldn't recognize normal in a Walmart."

Eric interrupted. "Before you two start playing another game of one-upmanship, I have a problem for you. We can't find any current chatter on the government coming after us. What do you make of it, Sarah?"

Sarah sat down in a chair and flipped her hair over her shoulder. "I'm the one who hit a wall in Washington. I'm not sure I have any input that helps. Nothing's out there?"

"Nothing," George said.

"Hmm. Possibly they're reloading their artillery and waiting for our response to Ms. Koole. If we go with the Mossad proposal, they don't fire. If we don't, they blow the house down."

"Exactly," Eric said. "That's what I've been thinking."

"One thing's for sure," George said. "My computer networks have an expansive reach. I don't think I've missed anything." He scratched his head.

"Sarah, anything turn up on what this Mossad agent might be working on?" Eric asked. "George ran several approaches to the problem but couldn't get past the firewall at the Mossad offices. I know Dan hasn't come up with anything more than that Koole worked in the Middle East and speaks Hebrew, Arabic, Farsi, German, and English. Beyond that, we know nothing."

Sarah shook her head.

Eric sighed. "I guess I have no alternative but to call Koole and tell her we accept the offer and expect all attacks by the US government to stop."

George shrugged. "What else can we do except head for South America and hide?"

Eric pulled out his cell phone. "Here goes." He began punching in numbers.

⬧⬧⬧

Simone sat in the kitchen of her Washington apartment drinking coffee when the phone rang. She had given Eric Stone the number of a cell phone purchased just for this one phone call.

"Hello," she said.

"We accept your offer," Stone said.

"Thank you."

"You can call off the US government's dogs."

"Done." Simone hung up.

Walking to the trash can, she smiled and dropped the cell phone in the container.

She picked up another cell phone.

"*Erev tov*," the man answered.

"The chase is on."

"Ah! The dragon man will be pleased."

"Where are you?"

"I am waiting to board the plane for Israel. You caught me at just the right moment."

"Have a good trip. I'll be in touch tomorrow."

"Shalom."

Simone went back to the kitchen table and finished her coffee.

14

Ebrahim Jalili followed the distinguished research scientist down the long cement tunnel sequestered three hundred feet underground the Natanz facility. The whirl of turbines blowing fresh air in expelled any musty smell lingering in the long hallway. A well-kept secret, the chamber at the other end had already been prepared to receive the new centrifuges that would enrich plutonium.

"We believe no one knows that we built this enlarged laboratory that has now been expanded to contain the new units that should arrive shortly," the nuclear physicist said. "We are secure."

"One can never be too careful," President Jalili said. "Spies have their own way of turning up in the most unexpected places. Trust no one."

The scientist nodded and unlocked the door at the end of the corridor. "See." He pointed across the large room already humming with 984 centrifuges spinning night and day. "We will immediately be able to accommodate the new shipment."

Jalili smiled. "Our Supreme Leader al-Hashemi will be

pleased. You can expect an ample reward when this project is complete."

The scientist paused for a moment. "You realize what this means?"

Jalili nodded.

"We will be in a position to make a nuclear device immediately. Does that give you pause to reflect, Mr. President?"

"Not for a moment. We are on our way to the top. We will immediately become the dominant power in the region. The Saudis will have to back away, and the Iraqis will bow in deference." He smiled broadly. "And the nation of Israel will be past history, buried beneath a pile of radioactive rubble."

◈-◈-◈

Simone knew the night flight to Israel had landed in Tel Aviv. Benny Gantz would be on his way to the Mossad office. Nothing proved easy in the Middle East, but her efforts had paid off this time. Every detail had unfolded as she had planned.

Simone picked up the *Washington Post* and surveyed the headlines before turning to the international news. After a quick read, she turned to the *New York Times* and looked for more details. Simone read world news intently when communiqués from the Office were not available or delayed. Finally, she folded the paper. She started to drop the newspapers in the trash can, but it was full. She pulled the plastic liner from the stainless steel container, tied the bulging bag, and walked out the back door. The narrow brick pathway led to a large garbage dumpster in the alley that ran behind the residences. She liked the area because the streets always remained quiet.

No one knew their neighbors, and that worked well for her. The street had a pleasant, gentle atmosphere that felt peaceful. Raising the lid, she dropped the sack into the container.

A deafening roar blasted through the air. Simone's body lifted off the ground and slammed into the dumpster. Pieces of debris flew past. Fire exploded overhead. Simone tried to cover her face, but chunks of wood bounced off her head. Smoke descended, causing her to cough violently.

The entire house had burst into flames; a million chunks of glass hurled across the backyard. Black clouds of smoke overshadowed the neighboring houses and darkened the backyard. In a matter of minutes, the second floor would collapse. Only then did she realize she couldn't hear.

Simone struggled to get to her feet, but dizziness dropped her to the ground. A warm sensation trickled down her cheek. She reached for her forehead and felt a deep cut. The distant sounds of crackling, burning wood slowly returned.

From somewhere, a fire engine's siren began to roar. Firefighters were coming, and the property would start crawling with police. Cops would ask a million questions that she couldn't afford to answer. They must not find her. Once again, she forced herself to stand up.

Walking down the alley proved more difficult than anticipated, but by the time she got to the end of the block, the dizziness had faded. The cut on her head now seemed to be more surface than serious. Simone stopped to catch her breath. Her blouse had been shredded and her jeans ripped. She probably looked like a runaway from a car wreck.

The sound of fire trucks coming to a halt and the shouts of men behind her rang through the air. In the middle of the next block, Simone realized she had been fleeing without any destination in mind. She needed a destination. Any destination. Some nameless motel would work for the day. The houses abutting the alley looked fuzzy. She forced herself to keep walking.

The thundering eruption must have destroyed everything in the house. Mossad documents and the computer in the bedroom would have burned. Nothing remained that would identify her.

Three blocks later, Simone dropped to the curb. Had a hot water tank exploded? A gas line ruptured? She wiped the blood from her cheek and gently felt the cut near her hairline. The obvious began to sink in; her mind started to clear. This wasn't a malfunction of some household appliance. She had barely escaped a bomb intended to kill her.

Could be a terrorist she'd once chased or a payback. Maybe her profile had become too visible in the Middle East, and an enemy of Israel simply wanted to take her out. No question about the explosion. The enemy had marked her for assassination.

She needed to change her appearance. Dye her hair. New clothes.

Whoever set off the bomb would be long gone by now, and she might never know who did it. Dragon man would be snorting fire over this one for certain. One conclusion was inescapable. She had to get out of Washington undetected and let the killer think the blast had blown her into a thousand pieces. She needed new clothes and an airplane ticket. But where to? Which street should she take next? Where would she go?

15

The week following Eric's telephone conversation with Dar Dagan in Tel Aviv, George continued his computer assessment of their vulnerability, but nothing filtered through. Eric followed the situation each day, but the lack of intel confounded him.

Jack walked into Eric's office. "Boss, I'm packed and on my way to Afghanistan." He sat down in the padded office chair across from Eric. "I'll fly from Denver to Frankfurt, Germany, before changing planes. Got to make several stops. Then on to Kabul."

"We'll miss you helping us sort out this situation with Simone Koole," Eric said. "But I'll look forward to receiving your updates."

"You'll get the first one soon after I land."

"Good." Eric extended his hand. "Keep safe."

"Me?" Jack laughed. "You're the one I worry about."

"I hope we have this confusion resolved by the time you hit Kabul, but I wouldn't bet on it."

"Let me know if the bombs start falling and I'll keep traveling to Japan."

"Yeah, if you don't hear from me again, you can guess I'm hiding under a rock in the Canadian arctic."

Jack slung a backpack over his shoulder, gave a quick good-bye salute, and left.

Eric walked back to George's office. George sat hunched over a keyboard with his thick glasses perched on the edge of his nose.

Sarah strolled in while surveying a printout. Her silk silver jacket hung over brown leatherette jeans etched from her ankles to her waist with swirling gray vines and flower designs. Long leather fringe edged the seam of her pants and swayed as she walked.

"Found something we should look at," she mumbled under her breath.

George looked up. "Hey, look, the rodeo queen just rode in."

Sarah looked at him disdainfully. "You never had much taste, you know."

"Yeah, but then again, I never came to work looking like a cross between Broadway and South Texas."

"Okay, okay," Eric interrupted. "Let's cut the bull and focus on business. What's up, Sarah?"

"I was catching up on reading and stumbled across this article about an explosion in Washington DC. Seems a house got blasted, and the police think a terrorist did it."

"I saw that story," George said with disinterest that bordered on boredom. "You ought to stick to the fashion section. It's more up your alley."

"You should be more observant, George. Speculation from an unidentified source thought it might have been an Israeli woman living there, but they were still trying to piece the story together. The story said the explosion might have been an attack on Mossad. Ring any bells?"

"A story like that doesn't leak out by accident," Eric said. "Something's going on."

"I immediately thought about Ms. Koole. Could be?"

"George, check out this story," Eric said. "If anything has happened to our Israeli spy, we need the details."

George began tapping words into his computer. Sarah and Eric watched over his shoulder. In a matter of seconds, a police report emerged on the screen.

"Looks like the Washington police definitely think it was sabotage," Sarah read.

George settled back in his chair. "I'll keep an eye on this story today."

"Do that," Sarah said. "Since it's your job anyway." She winked at Eric and strolled out.

⊰⊱ ⊰⊱ ⊰⊱

Simone stopped her car on the side of Evergreen Lake and started walking. The local golf course edged the lake and ran along the trail leading to the Upper Bear Creek area. Like the many hikers tracking along the narrow path and through the surrounding woods, she looked like an average visitor, but her steps were labored and slow. The explosion had left its mark on her right leg and hip. The cut on her head had not healed, and she still felt tired. Nevertheless, she walked at a determined pace.

She had known pain many times. Growing up on the kibbutz, she knew the usual aches that a hard day of hoeing in the fields left. When she began training as a Mossad employee, rigorous exercise left her exhausted and covered with bruises. Extra hours in the martial arts slammed her into the mats a million times and made her body feel woefully twisted out of shape. Simone had taken every hit with her teeth gritted and no excuses offered. The instructors always pushed new trainees to their limits, but she was determined never to utter a sound of protest. Simone watched their eyes and saw the hidden surprise when she didn't utter a moan. By the time she was inducted into Mossad, Simone knew she had earned the respect of the entire staff. That was all she wanted: respect.

"Good afternoon," an older lady said as she walked past.

"Good afternoon to you," Simone replied.

"Oh, my dear! You've injured your head."

"Oh, it's nothing." Simone picked up the pace.

Nothing wrong with people speaking, but she didn't want to be observed. At the end of the path, she cut through the bushes and into the forest.

Hidden in the forest up Bear Creek, the Conundrum's offices were located in one of the plush areas of the canyon. Along the winding highway stood a magnificent home towering over the creek that eventually emptied into the large lake. Even though the steep mountainside made walking difficult, Simone stayed covered by the trees and brush. The hike pained her injured leg, but she believed strenuous exercise would work out the aching. If not, she'd simply endure the strain.

Low branches swished across her face when she failed to duck, but Simone kept her eyes trained on what might emerge ahead of her. It was important that no one see her approach. After a three-mile walk, she came to a high fence. Walking along the fence, she soon found an indentation and quickly scooted under the wire. Once inside the property, she took out a small black electronic device that Mossad had supplied. Unknown outside of the agency, the device allowed an agent to block surveillance signals.

Sitting on the ground, Simone began sweeping the area with her sensor blocker. Slowly moving her arm from left to right, holding the black box, Simone crept through the trees.

Her device identified where sensors were located by blinking a red light and a dial with an arrow indicating direction. This allowed her to walk around the identified devices. However, the electronic box had the capacity to block any sense of movement that would trigger an alarm. The task she faced was moving slowly enough not to jam the system. If she did, the Conundrum staff would be all over her.

For thirty minutes, Simone edged through the trees until the house came into view. Once again, she lay flat and surveyed the area. To her surprise, she discovered a two-foot gap between the sensors that covered the front and back of the house.

She hurried down the two-foot gap. Within seconds, she stood on the ground floor of the house. She pulled out her fountain pen pick set and looked at the various small tools. She extracted a tension wrench and poked it into the keyhole and jiggled it back and forth. After a moment of twisting, the dock lock popped open. Simone smiled and pushed the sliding door open. She'd sit at the end of the long mahogany table and wait for Stone to appear. Nothing like a little surprise.

⋄⋄⋄

In the late afternoon, Eric walked up the stairs to the ground floor of his estate. He turned down the long hallway that joined the formal dining room to the large kitchen. He abruptly caught his breath. A red-haired woman sat at the head of the long mahogany table. She had a bandage on her forehead, and her face looked tired and drawn.

"Simone Koole?"

"Ah, so you recognize me."

"How did you get in here?"

"Mr. Stone, I'm an expert in surveillance systems."

"I thought . . . well, we wondered . . . there was an explosion in Washington."

"Unfortunate," Simone Koole said. "But we all have our little challenges."

"Then that was your house?"

"Belonged to my landlord. Looks like he gets to build a new one."

Eric slid into the large chair at the opposite end of the table. "You have an amazing way of showing up and disappearing."

"Let's stick to business," Simone said. "We have a lot to talk about today."

"You know who bombed your residence?" Eric asked.

"Not at this time, but we're working on it. We'll find them."

"You're aware that we checked you out?"

"Of course. Find any problems?"

"None."

Simone smiled. "Just as I told you."

"Judging by that patch on your forehead, I'd say you were injured in the blast."

"Only a scratch, but obviously someone's been on my trail. I'm always cautious, but the bar has been raised. I changed the color of my hair and made some other adjustments. You didn't recognize me at first glance."

"We have a better security system than the White House," Eric said. "You're the first to slip through."

"Of course," Simone said. "Now, moving on with the business at hand. I want you to assemble your staff. I am ready to discuss the next step in our operation."

"Everyone?"

Simone raised an eyebrow. "Every last one of them."

16

Gaining the upper hand topped Simone's list of priorities. Today the Conundrum team would accept that she ran the show. They would learn to respect her whether they liked it or not.

Dan Morgan sauntered by, assessing her out of the corner of his eye with a suspicious stare. Simone knew the look meant she didn't appear to be what he expected. Okay. Men always proved easier to mesmerize.

"Howdy," Morgan said in a squeaky voice that made him sound like a little cowboy wannabe.

Simone smiled even though the boyish voice didn't match the Superman muscles on his arms.

Sarah Fleming's long-legged stride conveyed confidence and certainty. Her expensive silver jacket and leather fringed pants made a striking statement and a clear contrast with Simone's plain cotton pullover. Simone studied the woman's contoured and dramatic eyes. A hint of disdain and superiority hung over Sarah Fleming. Mossad research had said Sarah didn't like competition. The casual, indifferent flip of her hair over her shoulder added to Simone's suspicions.

George Powers's thick glasses made him look like an owl scanning her. He watched her with his hands casually folded over his protruding stomach, but she sensed his mind was working overtime. Many people would be intimidated by George's magnified eyes the size of golf balls. Old cuddly George would probably turn out to be a teddy bear.

Simone watched Eric Stone slip into the chair at the other end of the table. He appeared compliant, but that initial appearance was only meant to deceive. She guessed Eric could only be pushed so far before digging in his heels.

He pulled a pen from his shirt pocket and looked around the room slowly. "Our colleague Jack Javidi usually sits with us, but this morning he's on his way to the Middle East. The floor is yours, Ms. Koole."

"Thank you, Mr. Stone," Simone said, matching his formality. "Mr. Javidi will be missed, but we will get by. We will all know each other very well before this task is completed. Let's keep it on a first-name basis. Just call me Simone. And, Eric, turn that SGB camera off. You flipped it on when we began the meeting. I didn't say anything in the restaurant, but from now on, no recordings of my face by any of you. Got it?"

No one spoke.

"The project you are now involved in is known as Digital Damage," Simone began. "Expect certain aspects of the operation to be time consuming. Some of you will be involved only at key points along the way. You will know nothing of the ultimate objective and will be informed of your participation only at the moment of need. I can assure you that what we are doing will prove vital for world peace."

"I'm a lawyer and an accountant," Sarah said. "I doubt you need my skills." The tone in her voice conveyed condescension.

She's testing me, Simone thought. *First round. Here we go.*

"We will, eventually," she said with a hardness in her voice.

Dan raised his hand. "I work the night detail," he said. "I'm the brawn to George's brains. How do I fit?"

"Every one of you has a part, but George will be the anchor. I need his computer abilities first and foremost."

George blinked several times. "Me?"

"Yes, George," Simone said. "You're the heart of this operation for the moment. You'll find our task quite the challenge." She leaned back in the chair and looked around the room. "I have studied dossiers on each one of you. I know your strengths and your weaknesses."

Sarah sat forward in her chair. "I'm curious what kind of information you have." Challenge rang in her words.

"I know all about you, Sarah. You carry a Walther PPK-L in a shoulder holster under that cute little jacket you're wearing. You're good at crunching numbers and have an excellent legal background. Harvard Law School could have put you in a big-money firm. You go for the knock-your-eyes-out stunning look as a distraction. However, you can be arrogant and like to flaunt your attractiveness. You'll prance like a show horse every time you get the chance. Sound about right?"

Sarah's mouth dropped.

"You're highly competitive, Sarah. I like that. Just don't lock horns with me." Simone smiled. "You'll lose every time."

Sarah raised her eyebrows but said nothing.

"You, Eric, are the indomitable force that runs the entire

operation. Your unfortunate habit of making the headlines must stop until this project is completed. Any problems with that?"

Eric shook his head. "You're the boss, Simone."

Simone smiled thinly. "Okay. I believe we are ready."

17

Eric watched his employees silently file out of the room. They appeared stunned by Simone's brisk, impersonal briefing. Eric waited until the last person had filed out before shutting the door and taking a seat.

"I think you got everyone's attention."

Simone raised an eyebrow. "Oh? Where I come from we call that a staff meeting. No big deal."

"Well, we're not 'where you come from.'"

"I know where I am. The question is, do you have a problem with me being in charge?"

Eric took a deep breath and pursed his lips. "N-o-o," he said slowly. "It's just that we treat each other like family here."

"I don't. The only thing that matters with me is getting the assignment done. Whether someone likes it or not is irrelevant."

"Being abrasive isn't a problem?"

"Look. I'm here for one reason. I have a job to do and my mission is to make sure it comes off with no problems."

Eric rubbed his jaw thoughtfully. "You're an interesting

person, Simone. I've never seen Sarah Fleming at a loss for words."

Simone said nothing.

"I think we'd do better if we treated each other like colleagues, friends, and—"

"Thank you for your opinion, Mr. Stone. But I don't operate that way. In my country we don't have time for niceties. Each day, we must be concerned for our survival. When Israel was born on May 14, 1948, the Egyptians attacked Tel Aviv with Spitfire bombers. We never forget we began in a state of war that has never stopped."

"I thought I was dedicated to my job and my country, Simone, but you do me one better."

"I try."

Eric stretched his legs under the table. "Hmm. Tell me more about what you believe in."

"My mother's parents died in Auschwitz and my father's parents fought in the Warsaw Ghetto. My father was shot because he refused to retreat from his right to live in Israel. We have always been people of the Book, and I remain so. You cannot separate Israel from the Torah. The God of ancient Israel chose us to walk through this world as his faithful servants. I serve him relentlessly."

"I see," Eric said thoughtfully.

"Your God is so different?"

"I grew up in the Christian faith. My parents took me to church. But as I told you earlier, my allegiance belongs to the righteous purposes of the United States of America. My commitment is to the freedoms and ideals this country enjoys, and I will allow no person or nation to steal those dreams."

"Then, you can understand that I must allow nothing to stand in the way of achieving my objectives. We will have no problem as long as we both remember our mutual goals." Simone stood up and turned toward the door. "I have work that must get done immediately. Anything else?"

He shook his head. "I understand where you're coming from. By the way, even if I don't agree with your impersonal approach, I admire your commitment."

⸙⸙⸙

Eric understood little of what Simone had said when she instructed George about the design of the computer storage device. Her Operation Digital Damage scheme demanded a small gizmo whose purpose only she understood. Even George seemed mystified. All they knew was that other experts in Europe were working on the same problem.

Only minutes before she departed, Simone had given him a large brown envelope meticulously sealed and an airline ticket for Stuttgart, Germany. She offered no hints of what the package contained.

"Just take it," Simone had said. "You'll know what you need to know when you need to know."

Now, sitting in a KLM Boeing 767 airliner, Eric felt a little like a puppet dancing at the whims of the puppeteer. Then again, what alternative did he have?

Eric thought about how strange the last week had been. One day the agency was making plans to flee the country, and the next, an Israeli spy was running the company. The only good aspect was that they were still in business and had survived a serious legal threat.

Eric yawned. The evening flight should give him good rest. He closed his eyes, pulled the wool blanket around his neck, and settled in for the night.

⋄⋄⋄

The morning sunlight bounced off the airplane's wing as they came to a halt at the Stuttgart airport's gate. Eric quickly gathered up his shoulder bag.

He had cleared passport control when he noticed an odd-looking character standing on the other side. The man fell in behind him. Eric lined up with the rest of the passengers to pull his bag off the carousel. The man stayed one hundred feet away but kept his eyes glued on Eric. Too much attention to be an accident. Eric studied the shabby brown jacket covering a T-shirt with a skeleton on the front. The guy had spiked black hair that stuck up like a hairbrush, and he looked strange particularly because his facial features were Middle Eastern. His dark skin and eyes didn't match the punk look. Maybe he was a wannabe; maybe not.

Eric pulled his bag off the conveyor and started walking. He passed through customs and started down the hall. Through a large glass window, he observed Mr. Spiky Head coming out of customs right behind him.

Eric darted around a corner in the tax-free zone. Watching from a perfume store, he observed Mr. Spiky Head not missing a step. No question. The guy was following him.

Outside the terminal, Eric grabbed a taxi and watched. Like clockwork, his tail grabbed the next cab.

"Bruder Haus Hotel," Eric told the driver.

"Okay," the man said and didn't look back.

Eric kept watching the taxi behind them. As had been the case in the terminal, the taxi stayed at a safe distance. Eric's driver slowed and pointed at a large ornate building across the street.

"This is it," he said.

"*Danke.*" Eric slipped money over the seat. "Let me out here."

Jumping to the curb, Eric watched as the other taxi rolled past. The tail had slumped against the backseat, making it impossible to see him clearly. Registering as Ethan Smith, the name that Simone had provided, Eric settled into his room. The spacious quarters had been decorated in a baroque style with all the flourishes. The luxury of such superb accommodations added an unexpected touch of class to the operation. To his surprise, a letter addressed to him lay on the desk. He picked it up cautiously and sniffed for any suspicious odor. He sliced it open.

Mr. Smith,

Hopefully you have arrived without incident. Tomorrow morning you are to go to the Styman Company located on Muellerstrasse.

Any taxi driver will know the location. At their desk, ask for computer analyst Otto Langer. You will give him the package that I sent with you. Tell him nothing more than that the package is part of Operation Digital Damage. Return to the hotel and await further instructions.

Eric read the letter a second time. Simone still played these hide-and-seek games, but he knew she had to trust him at some level or she wouldn't have contacted him in the first place. One explanation remained. He could be killed at any moment and she didn't want loose information floating around that could fall into the hands of terrorists. Operation Digital Damage came with heavy-duty baggage . . . like Mr. Spiky Head.

Eric opened his luggage and took out the 9mm Glock pistol and a shoulder holster. He lay down on the bed and wondered how the guy had known he was coming.

❖ ❖ ❖

After a German breakfast heavy on the gravy, biscuits, and greasy sausage, Eric left the hotel and started his journey to the Styman Company. Again, Simone had been correct. His mention of the Styman name sent the driver flying off down the street. Eric kept the brown envelope inside his coat pocket next to the 9mm Glock pistol.

The Styman plant proved to be a block-long cement building with few windows and none on the first floor. Whatever Styman and Otto Langer were into, the operation had to be conducted behind locked doors and difficult access. One large Styman Company sign stood above the front door. That was it.

Eric walked in nonchalantly. Glass, expensive tile, but no clues as to what might be inside. An attractive blonde sat behind a long desk and didn't look up. The only other door appeared locked, and no one would get in until she gave them passage.

"*Guten Morgen*," Eric said.

The woman looked up and said in English with an accent, "May I help you?"

"I'm here to see computer analyst Otto Langer," Eric said. "Your business?"

"Personal, but Herr Langer is expecting me."

The woman picked up the phone. "Your name?"

"Ethan Smith."

After a few minutes and several conversations, the lady pushed a button on the phone. A security guard the size of a small mountain entered the room and beckoned for Eric to follow him. The burly guard led him up a flight of stairs and into a small conference room.

"Mr. Langer will be with you shortly."

The guard closed the door, and the click of a lock meant Eric wasn't going anywhere by himself. After five minutes the door opened again. A tall, thin man with graying hair walked in wearing a white lab coat. He walked briskly across the room and sat down on the opposite side of the conference table.

"Yes?" the man said, maintaining a stern face.

"Otto Langer?"

"The same."

"I'm Ethan Smith. Simone Koole sent me."

"And what project brought you here?"

"Operation Digital Damage."

Langer smiled for the first time. "Were you followed?"

"Yesterday. Didn't see any shadow men today."

Langer's countenance returned to the stern hard stare. "Our enemies are a crafty lot." He leaned over the table. "You have something for me?"

Eric pulled out the large brown envelope. "I believe this is what you were expecting."

Langer leaned over the table and grabbed the envelope. "I will return shortly."

Eric watched him hurry away. Apparently, whatever he was supposed to do had come off on schedule, but Eric still wasn't sure what was going on. Five minutes later, Otto Langer returned and handed the same brown envelope back to him.

"You will find the matter in order," Langer said.

Eric looked at the envelope that appeared just as it had when he had given it to the analyst.

"You will be leaving through a side entrance that leads straight to the subway. I would strongly suggest you take the train to the third exit. When you come out, you will be in a quiet neighborhood and not far from your hotel. Hopefully, no one will be following you. Leaving now would be best." Langer stood up. "Thank you for your efforts. You have greatly helped in a cause that we both love and support."

Eric assumed the man must mean Israel although he had never spoken the word.

Langer bowed slightly and left the room.

18

After hurrying down the steps outside the Styman Building, Eric found the metro entrance and boarded the subway. Otto Langer had insisted he should leave quickly. While Eric couldn't be sure, he assumed Langer had worried that Eric might be in danger.

The subway coach jerked back and forth while the train rambled down the bumpy track. The first exit came up quickly, and Eric watched the passengers getting on and off. No one said a word. The unspoken message was the same on subways around the world: "Don't bother me; I won't bother you."

Once again the train slowed, stopped, and another rush of passengers poured in. Each person appeared to be an average German citizen going about their business as indifferently as the first group. When the train slowed for the third exit, Eric edged to the door. The terminal emptied quickly while he studied the exits. Satisfied as to his security, he hurried up the stairs and walked through the final outlet that emptied into the street.

Langer's description proved accurate. The neighborhood appeared quiet, with few citizens walking the street. A young woman pushed a baby stroller down the opposite side of the street. A couple of cars zoomed past. His pocket map said the hotel would be two streets over and several blocks up. A short walk. Looked good.

Eric started breathing easier and slowed his pace. While the next stop in this strange journey remained a mystery, he expected new instructions would be waiting at the hotel. Eric pulled the brown envelope from under his coat and took a look. At first glance, the envelope seemed unchanged. Upon examination, he noticed a difference. The seal was the same, but the envelope felt thicker. Whatever had been inside had been switched.

Eric paused at the street corner and started to put the envelope in his pocket. A motorcycle's roar caught his attention. A motorcycle squealed toward him. Out of the corner of his eye, he saw two men in black leather jackets heading for him. The passenger riding on the back had his hand out to grab Eric. Swinging his shoulder and elbow at the man on the back, Eric knocked him into the street. His black helmet cracked against the pavement and bounced off. Eric immediately recognized the spiked haircut.

The motorcycle swung around in the street in a wide circle, but Mr. Spiky Head had already gotten up and was coming fast. Reaching under his coat for his Glock, Eric dropped to his knee to aim, but the man leaped through the air before Eric could get positioned. The two men hit the sidewalk and rolled off the curb into the gutter.

The attacker's leather gloves caught Eric's face with two solid blows. Eric tried to dodge but got a hard punch in the stomach. He tried to knock the assailant away, but the man's blows to his head left him woozy. He heard the motorcycle roaring and knew the other thug was on his way. Mr. Spiky Head brought up a knee aimed at Eric's groin but only caught him in the thigh. Eric's leg buckled and he tried to back away.

Spiky Head grabbed the brown envelope and ripped it away. The bike bounced up on the curb, and the driver swung a chain at Eric. The links caught his shoulder, but the end of the chain bounced toward the side of his head. He tumbled backward over a hedge and landed on the lawn between the sidewalk and an old house.

"Got it?" the driver yelled.

"Let's see what's in here," Spiky Head said.

Eric's vision blurred, and he realized blood was running into his eyes. He could do no more than lie in the grass and try to get his wits back.

Spiky Head cursed violently.

"Nothing?" the driver asked.

"He's got nothing! Maybe he's not the right guy."

"We need to get out of here," the driver demanded. "Police are going to show up."

The motorcycle roared to life, and Eric could hear it flying down the street. He waited until the sound died out and then tried to get up. His thigh ached and made it difficult to move, his eyesight remained fuzzy, and he couldn't catch his breath. He staggered through the hedge and back onto the street. People were beginning to gather and were pointing toward him. He couldn't stay around. Eric trudged to the curb. Blank sheets of paper were strewn all over the street. The brown envelope lay torn open near the drain. The attackers had found nothing but white paper. He grabbed the envelope, stuffed it in his coat, and began walking as fast as he could.

He staggered into the plush hotel, noting that people stepped aside as he walked toward the elevator. He looked down and realized his shirt had been ripped and the leg of his pants torn.

"Can we help you, sir?" A bellhop rushed to his aid. "You've been hurt."

"Got to get to my room," Eric muttered.

"But, sir . . ."

The elevator door opened and Eric stepped in. "I'm okay," he said as the door closed.

Once in his room, Eric limped into the bedroom and fell on the bed. His head throbbed and his thigh ached. After ten minutes, he dragged himself to the bathroom and started washing the blood from his face. The chain had opened a nasty gash in his scalp, but there wasn't time for a doctor. He had to get out of there.

Another note lay on the table in the same place where he had found the last one.

Mr. Smith,
    Your next stop is to return to Denver.
    There's no timetable for this trip. Leave when you are ready.
    Keep up the good work.

An airplane back to the USA would do fine. His head throbbed.

A little ice remained in the bucket on his nightstand. He

wrapped it in a towel. Holding it against his head, he tried to clarify his thoughts. He had the experience, the background, the training to do spy work, and yet this Israeli woman made him feel like a rank amateur. Eric stretched out on the bed with the towel pressed against his head. Exhaustion settled over him. He felt lucky to be alive.

19

The bench in Denver's expansive City Park wasn't particularly comfortable, but it would work. Trees swayed in the background behind Simone, and a slight hint of the scent of flowers floated by in the breeze. Colorado was eight hours behind German time. Otto Langer should have just arrived at his house. She punched a long string of numbers into her cell phone.

"*Ja*," a low German voice answered.

"Otto Langer?"

"Who's calling?"

"An old acquaintance from Tel Aviv."

"Ah!" Langer said. "How are you, my dear?"

"I'm fine if everything is okay with you, Otto."

"Quite so. Yes. I am excellent."

"You received the plans and data in good condition?"

"Yes. Very interesting adjustments you have made in the project. Your delivery man did his job and left immediately."

"Otto, we are making progress. I don't have to tell you how important this is."

"No, you certainly don't."

"Do you anticipate any problems with this assignment?"

"No. I understand what you want me to do. It will take awhile, but I will get the work done as soon as possible."

"Great," Simone said. "I'll be back in touch soon." She hung up.

Simone remembered meeting Otto ten years earlier during a gathering in Tel Aviv when he had been introduced to her as a colleague in the Zionist cause. Otto Langer had escaped the Holocaust because his birth family gave him to German Christians who were sympathetic with the plight of the Jews. Meir Goldman never knew his original name until after he had turned twenty-one. By then, he had become a distinguished student at Heidelberg's Institute of Science, where he later pioneered much of Germany's early work on computers. While he kept the Langer name, he became an ardent supporter of the state of Israel. Private conversations led Simone to divulge Israel's need for computer expertise, and soon Otto Langer had become a secret colleague in the cause of defeating terrorism. Simone had no doubt that Otto had succeeded in the task she sent him.

She dialed another number. "*Boker tov*," a woman answered.

"I need to speak to Dar Dagan."

"May I ask who is calling?"

"Simone Koole."

The phone went silent.

"Allo," a man's gruff voice said.

"You're working late tonight?" Simone asked.

"Ha-ha." Dagan's voice conveyed no emotion. "What do you want?"

"I thought that I should let you know that the Digital Damage project is moving along on schedule."

After a long pause, Dagan said, "I know you didn't call just to give me this little update. You want to know if we've caught whoever blew up your residence."

"Now that you mention it, that has been on my mind. I understand your boys don't operate as fast as I do."

"Don't sound so smug. Of course, we have made progress."

"And who might we be talking about?"

"Remember that little hit job on al-Mabhoub in Dubai?"

"A woman doesn't talk about her little secrets."

"Nevertheless, it put you up near the top of Hamas's must-kill list."

Simone squirmed. She hadn't anticipated this turn in the conversation. "You don't say."

"Seems Hamas has gotten a little more ambitious and international. They sent one Abd al-Rashid to take care of the problem of Simone Koole. He found a way to get into your basement and wire up an explosive device that blew the house into a million pieces."

"Abd al-Rashid?" Simone mumbled.

"Forget the name," Dagan said. "He had an accident in Rome. The newspapers say he apparently fell down a steel staircase in the airport while flying back to Dubai. Nobody knows how it happened, but there is a rumor he might have been pushed. He won't be making any more trips looking for you. Our last reading from an informant indicated Hamas now believes al-Rashid destroyed you in the house bombing, so you're no longer on the must-kill roster."

"How nice. Any other news I should know?"

"Hundreds of Syrians have run for Lebanon to avoid President Bari's troops. Bari sent tanks to surround Hama when funerals began for sixty-five protestors gunned down the day before. How's that for a picture of benevolence? The Syrian army killed who knows how many. We guess around a hundred soldiers have been shot and no small number of police died. Bari calls the opposition militant Islamists and provocateurs. He didn't even name Israel as part of the current problem. Interesting tidbit?"

"Syria and Lebanon always try to export their problems to Israel. American newspapers noted busloads of discontented Palestinians were transported to the Israel border for protests. Couldn't have happened without the opposition government's approval."

Dagan chuckled. "Syrian residents in Deraa recently shouted at television cameras that they hoped the Israelis would occupy them because our soldiers are far more humane than their own Syrian army."

"What would you think if Bari was overthrown?" Simone asked.

"The devil you know has to be preferred to the devil you don't know."

"Okay," Simone said. "Got the picture. I'm signing off."

"Be sure and destroy the phone."

"Of course. I'll be back in touch, dragon man."

"Do that, and quit calling me that name."

"Good-bye."

Simone hung up and began disassembling the cell phone. She pulled the SIM card out and slipped it in her pocket. She started back up the street and dropped the pieces in a trash can. A block away, she tossed in the SIM card.

20

The return flight from Stuttgart landed thirty minutes early due to winds blowing in their favor. Immediately upon arrival, Eric called Dan Morgan to pick him up. He slowly exited the airplane, still dragging his leg. The airport tram took Eric into Denver International's terminal. When Dan's black Ford Escort pulled up to the curb, Eric eased himself in.

"You look like you've been hit by a train."

"A couple of guys jumped me on a backstreet in Stuttgart. Wasn't exactly the highlight of my trip."

Dan worked his way through the traffic driving toward the I-70 expressway to return to the mountains.

"Got an email from Jack," Dan said. "He arrived in good shape and has already gone to work. Seems as if the Taliban's not fighting the war right now. They're all out harvesting poppy plants to start next year's opium market rolling again."

"Slightly contradicts Senator Rassmussen's latest statement that the Taliban is in retreat because of USA armed pressure," Eric said. "If confronted, Rassmussen would say it's the same story, just different slants. Right?"

Dan shook his head. "Always the same old story. Razzle-dazzle the public. Keep the home folks smiling regardless of the truth."

"We're in business to keep people like the good senator honest. I try to think of it as job security. Jack have anything else to say?"

"He thinks we've turned the tide and the Taliban continues to take it on the chin. Jack's more optimistic than he's been in the past."

"Good news," Eric said. "We can use the positive reports."

"One other matter," Dan said. "Simone Koole arrived unexpectedly earlier this morning. She's at the compound waiting for you."

"Great," Eric said in an exasperated voice. "She's all I need. Another headache on top of this headache. Another round with her ought to finish me off after a long, long night of no sleep. I think I'll take a nap."

❖ ❖ ❖

Eric set his suitcase against the wall and stared at Simone Koole once again sitting at the other end of the long mahogany table in the formal dining room. In plain blue jeans and a purple crochet appliqué top, she looked more hip than usual. Her dyed red hair hung loosely over her neck. The harsh stare had gone out of her eyes.

"Other than getting your head stuck in the door, you've done a good job so far," Simone said.

"Oh, really?" Eric's voice carried a sardonic twist. "Any moron could have done the same until the firing squad picked up my trail coming out of the Styman Building. You didn't

110

tell me some guy with a bad hairstylist was going to try to kill me."

"You're a pro. I figured you could handle yourself."

"I appreciate your confidence."

Simone smiled. "The important thing is that you pulled it off with panache. Took a couple of licks, got on the airplane, and came home with mission accomplished. In our business, that's all that matters."

"Could have used some of that divine intervention you're so sure about. How do you think God feels about this mission?"

"We're doing well. I'd say *Adonai* would be pleased with us."

"*Adonai*, huh?" Eric shrugged. "I'm afraid I don't see world events in that light. Terrorists explode bombs. Nations implode. People are cruel. National leaders act like three-year-olds. As the bumper stickers say, 'Stuff happens.' My job is to protect the USA. That's where I pledge my allegiance."

"You should read your Bible more often. The book of Job tells us that *HaShem* makes nations great and destroys them as well. He enlarges and tears down. If I were you, I'd bet on his side of the table."

Eric gently touched his welts where the attacker had punched him. "I'm a little on the slow side, having been worked over by a jackhammer. Sorry. Lying there in the streets of Stuttgart, I didn't quite feel like the Almighty was working *that* hard for my side."

"Here you are alive when you could be dead and you don't recognize that as a miracle?"

"Miracle?" Eric snorted. "Clue me in, Simone. Just what are we building in all of this secret stuff that you're hiding from me?"

She smiled again. "It's all part of a divine puzzle to protect the world from the terrorists. I cannot tell you more now, but you will eventually see the importance of each piece of the puzzle. It is the hand of God that keeps these maniacs and their supporters from killing us."

Eric crossed his arms over his chest. "Tell me, Simone. Do you hate the Arabs? Are the Muslims your enemy?"

"I grew up with Arab Muslims. I have friends who are Muslims."

"I'm not sure that I understand your answer. Aren't you at war with Arabs?"

"Israel is not," Simone said emphatically. "We are at war with Muslims who love death more than life. It makes no difference what their religious background may be, our battle will always be with anyone who uses death as a weapon to destroy righteous people. Suicide bombers that kill innocent women and children violate the principle of life that we live by. Such indiscriminate killers are our enemies, and we must fight them in every possible way until they are completely eliminated."

"So, you're not fighting Muslims and Arabs in general?"

"Of course not! Our problem is with those who love death and refuse to join the effort to protect life. We must oppose groups that cultivate the demons of hate. These snakes kill innocent children. They would prefer to die trying to annihilate our people than live in harmony with the rest of the world. I believe that our God wants us to stop this onslaught of death."

"How about evil, Simone. Is the devil bearing down on us?"

"Jews have a different view of evil, Eric. We don't believe

112

evil has an independent power base on its own. *HaShem*, or God as you would say, can use evil to test and improve us. However, if we fail to recognize the trial for what it is, then evil can use us in wicked ways. Our enemies could be our friends and we could live peacefully side by side. Unfortunately, they have fallen prey to evil and are now attempting to destroy us."

Eric settled back in his chair. "Simone, you amaze me. I've never known anyone who was as tenacious and skillful an espionage agent as you are while being so religious."

"You are no different, Eric. You have laid your life on the line to protect America because you passionately believe in the ideals of your country. Perhaps you will find a deeper meaning in your work. I place a high value on your tenacity and spirit. Don't worry. We will prevail."

Eric gently patted the wound beneath his hair. "My head hopes so."

21

Eric strolled into George's office, stepping carefully around computers, printers, cables, and gadgets piled around the junked-up room. George was hammering away on a computer keyboard, completely lost in the project at hand. He never liked being interrupted, so Eric watched him silently, trying not to distract.

Sarah walked in reading a printout and accidentally stumbled over a spool of wire, sending a bang echoing across the room.

George jumped. "Huh!"

"Easy," Eric said. "I've been standing here for several minutes. Didn't want to disturb you."

"Well, Ms. Fashion Parade certainly didn't have that problem."

Eric glanced at Sarah's rather provocative white lace top and elaborate silver belt buckle fastened to white jeans with blue flowers spiraling up the pant legs.

"Okay, okay," Eric said. "What's going on, Sarah?"

"I've been checking our foreign bank accounts. Some outside source recently broke in and monitored our funds in

Switzerland. They didn't take anything. Just took a look. Apparently, the hackers simply wanted to know how much we had in that particular account. The bank is upset that they broke through their firewall."

George snatched the page out of Sarah's hands. "Let me see."

"Notice," Sarah said to Eric, "how genteel George always is. Sort of like a pig peeling a banana."

"You two are going to kill each other someday. Why don't you go back and work on how that hacker broke in and I'll keep George happy."

Sarah nodded. "Sure." She looked at George and rolled her eyes. "See ya around, sweetie." She left.

"I swear the two of you are worse than kindergarteners," Eric said. "You go at each other every time you're in the same room."

A grin crossed George's face. "I have to keep her in line or she'd drive us all crazy."

Eric raised an eyebrow. "Yeah, George. Maybe you ought to find a hobby like fishing." He leaned over and spoke more softly. "What are you working on for Simone?"

George shook his head. "Strangest thing I ever saw. She wants me to construct a USB storage device that will carry two contradictory messages at the same time. Never done that before. I'm not sure what's going on, but the USB device material you took to Stuttgart contained what I've developed so far. Apparently, she's going to attempt to tie into some system with two sets of instructions that normally would cancel each other out. And she wants it all in a small package. That's quite a task. It looks like we're developing both a program as well as a device to carry it. Some German guy is going to add an additional component, but what the entire process accomplishes escapes me. I don't have a clue what she's up to."

"Picking up any more data on if the CIA still has us in their sights?"

George shook his head. "Just as quiet on that front as a morgue."

Eric walked out and returned to his office. Whatever Simone Koole had in mind continued to elude him.

22

Darkening clouds and threatening rain hung over the towering mountains. Simone drove slowly on the descending I-70 stretch from Evergreen into Denver; a speeding ticket might end up betraying her identity. Her identity and location had to stay under wraps until the Digital Damage assignment had been completed.

Simone kept thinking about Eric Stone. In all her years with Mossad, he was the first American who had asked her what she believed. Eric Stone was different. He didn't spit out meaningless words. The man put his life on the line and his fortune behind his convictions. While he said the destiny of America was his god, she could read between the lines. Perhaps he blurred ethical considerations because that's what intelligence work demanded, but she could sense he had more convictions about the reality of the God who created the universe than he had expressed. It was only a hunch, but she sensed he had ethical values rooted in a faith.

A Porsche whizzed by, but Simone didn't speed up. She had one objective today that she hadn't told Eric or anyone else about. She was moving her operation to Denver.

In the beginning of her work with Mossad, she had learned that a moving target was much harder to hit. By shifting locations, she made herself less visible. How had that man who had bombed her house found her? She still didn't know. And the attack on Eric in Stuttgart. How had those guys gotten into this hide-and-seek game? She didn't know that either, but that was part of the spy business. People showed up out of nowhere and didn't introduce themselves. Moving to Denver would be good cover. Nobody would expect a Mossad agent in Denver.

At the edge of the Arvada suburb, Simone pulled off the highway and drove down Ward Street. The apartment listed in the *Denver Post* sounded good. Simone studied the old brick facade across the front of the long apartment. Genuine seventies. Transitional neighborhood. It would work.

She knocked on the manager's door. An old woman with dyed jet-black hair that looked like a fuzz ball opened the deteriorating door a crack and peered out.

"Yeah?"

Working hard to cover any accent, Simone said, "You still got an apartment to rent?"

The woman swung the door open wider. "Sure. Come in."

Looking to be in her late sixties, the woman had a pear shape suggesting far more than one too many French fries with her last Happy Meal.

"I need a one-bedroom flat for at least six months."

"Got you covered, sweetie." The woman waddled toward a key rack hanging on her living room wall and picked up a single key. "Follow me." She shuffled past Simone. "I'll show you the apartment. Furnished, you know."

Simone fell in behind her. Six units down, the woman unlocked the door. The granny flat had a single couch in the living room and a lone double bed in the bedroom. The small kitchenette held only basics.

"One thousand dollars a month for this one."

Simone glanced around the room. The joint smelled like a stale attic. "I'll give you $750."

The woman's mouth twisted nervously. "Eight hundred is the best I can do. Includes utilities, you know."

"Okay." Simone reached for her purse. "I pay in cash. Any problem?"

"Money's money." The woman held her hand out.

Simone counted out eight one-hundred-dollar bills. The woman's eyes danced.

"My, my."

"You can expect the same on the first day of every month."

The woman nodded. "Good. We're in business." She dropped the key into Simone's hand. "By the way, what did you say your name was?"

"Alicia," Simone said. "Alicia Bernardo."

"Well, we don't sign any leases around here. Paying your rent on time covers it. Just don't try to steal any of the furniture or I'll call the cops."

"Wouldn't think of it." Simone's fingers tightened around the key. "See ya."

The woman trudged out the door, leaving Simone looking around the sparsely furnished apartment. A skip tracer might find this dump, but it wouldn't be easy. Consequently, Alicia Bernardo would be invisible. Getting utilities with the apartment eliminated registering with the city.

She looked out the front window. She'd already made sure her new name wasn't listed on Intelius People Search. With a half dozen passports in her luggage and credit cards under a wide assortment of names, Alicia Bernardo shouldn't have a worry about that angle.

Simone sat down on the dilapidated bed and studied the room. Many times her life had felt like this apartment. Empty. No pictures on the wall. No comfortable chairs. No rug on the floor. A spartan room to chill out in while waiting for the next shoe to drop. Years of emptiness stretched into nothingness.

No one at the Conundrum organization would ever know about this apartment or that she was living in Denver. Intelligence work demanded secrecy that only added to a sense of hollowness. Such was the journey that *Adonai* had given her. She accepted it, but that didn't make it any easier. For a long time, Simone sat on the mattress staring at the empty wall.

Then, Eric Stone came to mind again.

23

Jack Javidi unbuckled his seat belt and prepared to exit into Baghdad International Airport. During the Gulf War and US-led invasion in 2003, he had wiggled in and out of the country many times to uncover the truth behind the head-lines and propaganda released by the government. Jack had always been impressed with American soldiers and respected their dedication.

He went through passport control, walked into the ter-minal, and headed for the exit. Battered taxis waited at the curb. He grabbed the first one and shoved Iraqi dinars into the driver's hand. "Get me downtown fast and I'll pay you well."

"Ah! A man of distinction," the driver said. He had only one front tooth remaining, and his deeply tanned, worn face had wrinkles in every corner. "Where does this leader of men want me to take him?" His wide grin also revealed only a few teeth remaining in the back of his mouth.

"Sheab Street."

"We are almost there already!" The driver rammed the

dirty two-decades-old Ford into the thick traffic. Sitting on his horn, he blared past the other cars and pushed his cab ahead of the pack.

Jack knew they were at least ten miles west of downtown, and the ride over the Tigris River via Yafa Street would be anything but fast. Still, he had the driver's attention.

Charred remains of the US-led war lay scattered on all sides. Debris filled backstreets, and nearly collapsed buildings lined the roads. Not much had changed since his last visit. The various tribes were still fighting their own little wars in the alleys.

Jack pulled out his notepad and began scribbling observations. Little escaped his notice, and most of it ended up filed somewhere between A to Z in his extensive filing system.

The taxi hooked up with Yafa Street and rumbled toward the bridge over the ancient Tigris. The driver jerked in and out of heavy traffic, jockeying for an advantage in the long line of cars trying to enter the downtown area. Jack figured he must have given the driver more money than he realized—and that his insurance policy better be current.

Many nations had fought over this spot. The Hulagu Khan brought the Mongol Empire in the twelfth century, killing somewhere between two hundred thousand and a million inhabitants of Baghdad. In the fourteenth and fifteenth centuries, the Ottoman Turkish Empire swept in, and a new regime descended on the city. World War I brought the British and with them Colonel Lawrence, *the* Lawrence of Arabia. The city had known little peace and must have been rebuilt a hundred times. The future repeated the past.

The cab bounced over seemingly bottomless potholes and

eventually turned into Shaikem Oman Street. Surprisingly, the center of the city had many tall buildings and appeared remarkably modern considering the war that had exploded in its streets.

"Where would you wish to stop?" the driver asked. "We are nearly to Sheab Street."

"After you turn to the right, go two blocks. I'll tell you where to stop."

"As you say, generous one."

The local boys never quit priming the pump, but Jack knew the tips, and a decent price meant the difference between life and death for a man with a family. Money didn't fall from the sky for the common people.

"Right here." Jack pointed to a sidewalk café. "Let me out."

"Of course."

Jack again pressed dinars into the man's outstretched hand. "Keep the change."

"Allah be blessed!" He drove away with a grin on his face.

Fifty feet away, an old acquaintance sat at an outdoor café table waiting for him. Jalai Usama had survived the various wars with everyone from the Iranians to the Americans. Old enough to know all the tricks of the trade, Jalai understood the inside of the inside of Iraq.

"My old friend!" Jalai immediately stood. "I am honored to have you return to our city."

Jack hugged him and they both exchanged kisses on each other's cheeks. Jack stood back and studied Jalai. The old scar on the man's neck bore witness to a fight years ago. His belly had begun to protrude and his clothes looked secondhand, but Jack knew the shopworn appearance was a strategy. Jalai kept a bankroll the size of Dallas.

"What brings my enterprising brother back to this god-forsaken part of the world?"

"I like to drop by periodically to make sure that my friend Jalai is alive and well. That's all."

The Arab shrugged. "To stay alive in Baghdad is an accomplishment. The Sunnis and Shiites keep trying to kill each other while the Kurds in the north run for cover. The government is incompetent and the politicians lie every minute of every day. Other than those small annoyances, life is fine."

Jack laughed. "Only you, Jalai, could put it so modestly."

"A coffee for my friend," Jalai called to a waiter.

"How is life in Iraq?"

Jalai shook his head. "The Americans still think they'll make us into a democracy. They're crazy. The average Iraqi has no idea what they are talking about. All we've ever known is chaos and cruel dictators. Saddam Hussein? Evil to the core. As soon as the Americans run out of money and get out of the picture, we'll go back to the likes of him." Jalai threw up his hands. "That's my opinion."

"How are things with your military?"

Jalai grinned. "Incompetent, but maybe you want to buy some guns? Explosives? Maybe a helicopter? You have come to the right man. If the price is right, I can supply the goods."

"A helicopter? You're not serious."

"What do you want? UH-1 Iroquois utility helicopter? An HH-60 Pave Hawk?" Jalai leaned over the table. "I can even put my hands on an AH-64 Apache attack unit—if you have that much money."

The waiter set a small cup of pitch-black coffee in front of Jack. The scent of the steam had the strength to singe one's nostrils.

"And how does my friend accomplish such things?"

"The Americans leave equipment lying around where we can pick it up. Some officers are more interested in money than the cause they fight for. I know who these people are."

"Sounds like the country isn't in particularly great shape these days. The American press turned its attention to Afghanistan. The public isn't hearing much about Iraq."

"Of course not. The news is boring. No missiles shooting fire into the night sky for the TV cameras. Who cares anyway?"

Jack knew Jalai didn't lie to him, and the man would press for the last possible dinar in a business deal. However, his assessments of life on the street were always accurate and timely.

"And the Iranians?" Jack asked.

"They filter in like summer mosquitoes. The pests are everywhere. Of course, Iran supports the Shiites and keeps their gun barrels aimed at politicians in this country. We must be cautious or they will initiate another war as soon as the American influence diminishes."

Jack nodded. "That's the picture I've been getting. Okay, my friend. What can I do for you today?"

"A little business would be nice. Perhaps you'd like to buy a case of M203 grenade launchers that can fit under an M16 rifle. I can even get you a box of M16s to go with them. Brand-new. Never been fired."

"Not to my taste today."

Jalai laughed. "I know the Conundrum will always come

125

to me first and you know I will have what you need. The right time will arrive. Let us drink our coffee and enjoy the day."

"Of course." Jack took a small sip of the strong coffee and quickly set it down.

24

In the time since Eric had returned from Europe, George had worked night and day attempting to perfect the computer assignment Simone Koole had given him, but nothing had worked. Still, George persevered.

That morning, he didn't notice Eric and Dan standing in his office watching him work.

"How's it going?" Eric finally said.

George jolted slightly before laying down a tiny soldering iron and wiping his forehead. "Tough one."

Dan nodded. "Yeah. What exactly are you trying to make?"

George ran his fingertips across his forehead. "I'm creating a 'worm' with the capacity to create chaos wherever it lands." He turned back to the soldering iron. "Making two contradictory programs operate at the same time ain't easy. I'm working on the program and a device at the same time."

He sighed. "The assignment is frying my brain. This worm I'm creating has to fit on a flash drive small enough to carry in your pocket. Other experts are working on additional aspects of the problem, but I have no contact with them."

"Koole doesn't even want you to email these other guys?" Dan asked.

"Nope. I'm locked in a closet by myself."

Dan shook his head. "Better you than me."

George snorted. "If you'll excuse me, boys, I've got to get back to work."

"Hang in there," Eric said. Putting his arm around Dan's shoulder, he pushed him toward the door. "Yell if you need anything." He laughed. "Though I don't have any idea how I'd help." He walked toward the steps leading upstairs. "Go back to reviewing the information received from Jack. I'll be in the kitchen."

"Sure." Dan walked away.

Eric hurried up the stairs and down the long hall. Maybe a little something from the refrigerator would be good right now. Delays made him nervous. George was always outstanding at what he did, but it was taking way too long to solve the puzzle Simone had given him. He opened the door on the refrigerator and reached in for the carton of milk.

"You thirsty?" a woman's voice said behind him.

Eric whirled around.

"Little nervous too?" Simone Koole said.

"How'd you get in here again?"

"I walked in."

"We updated our security since the last time you crawled through the maze. How'd you do it this time?"

"Call it a talent," Simone said.

Eric took a deep breath.

"We need to talk." Simone crooked her finger and beckoned. "Maybe you'd be more comfortable in the living room where we can enjoy the scenery while we chat." She walked out of the kitchen.

Eric followed along behind her. "No one should be able to get through what we've rigged up out there." Simone's black studded sweater hung below her waist, covering the top of her skinny jeans. Opaque buttons around the neck left a striking accent. Yes, he enjoyed the scenery.

Simone sat down on the leather couch that faced the long stone fireplace. "We need to have a little talk." She smiled. "Don't be so edgy, Eric. It's part of my job to be able to find my way through a security system. Keeps me on my toes to leap through your hoops. Good practice. Don't worry. I won't tell anybody."

Eric sat down opposite her in an overstuffed leather recliner. "We're not exactly amateurs in this business."

"Indeed. You wouldn't be working for me if you were."

"Okay, but I'd like to know when you're planning one of these little end runs. You drop in like a shadow, and it's a little disconcerting. No one has any idea where you live, where you fly in from."

Simone's smile had an alluring twist. "Let's get down to business."

Eric looked out the picture window. "Okay. What's up?"

"We need to go to England. I want Dan Morgan to go with us. We might need a strong arm. Last time you got messed up on a backstreet in Stuttgart. Let's cover all the bases this time."

"Dan always provides an excellent cover. No problem there."

"We'll be taking what Powers has created so far on a USB device. Make sure he keeps the original in your safe."

"I'll talk with George," Eric said thoughtfully. "Dan too. They'll need time to get ready."

"They don't have much time. I already have the airline tickets, so we have a deadline to meet."

"Well, just how much time do we have?"

"We will leave here in an hour."

Eric blinked several times and shook his head. "An hour?"

Simone got up and walked toward the door. "I'll be back for you in an hour. Be ready."

Eric watched her swinging gait glide across the room.

She stopped at the door, turned around, and smiled. "Don't be late."

25

London's Heathrow Airport bustled with passengers hurrying from one terminal to another. Blending into the crowd, Eric and Simone hustled toward passport control with Dan Morgan behind them. Nationals from India with passports in hand stood behind Nigerians standing across from Canadians and Australians. The three Americans lined up with the rest.

Using passports provided by Simone, Eric and Simone became Mr. and Mrs. George Flint on vacation from New York. Dan's passport declared him to be Don Morris, a businessman from Detroit. The British passport control officer stamped their documents without a hitch and sent them on their way. After grabbing luggage, cruising through customs, and hailing a black square-topped taxi, they sped off toward St. James Hotel located off Green Park and close to Buckingham Palace.

"So far, so good," Dan whispered to Eric.

"I'm sure we look like tourists taking in the sights," Eric said.

"You bet." Dan looked out the window at the buildings whizzing by. "Just sightseers."

The taxi pulled up in front of the historic hotel, and the driver hopped out to unload their luggage.

Simone handled the check-in, and a bellhop whisked them up to their rooms. The elevator quickly deposited them on the third floor.

"Simone and I will stay around here tonight," Eric told Dan. "I imagine you might like to take in the city. Feel free to do so. We don't start until the morning."

Dan nodded. "I think I might run up to the West End and take in a play. Something or the other." He kept walking down the hall to his room. "See you tomorrow at 8:00 a.m. sharp."

The bellhop had already opened the door to room 306 and placed their bags in racks beside the spacious closet. The room looked elegant and large. On top of the baroque desk, a computer and fax stood ready for their use. Two small couches faced each other in one corner across from beds covered with silk bedspreads.

"Everything suitable, sir?" the bellhop asked.

Eric slipped a couple of bills into the man's hand. "Fine. We're set. Thank you."

The bellhop bowed at the waist and hurried off.

"The English know how to do it right," he said to Simone. "My room is next door. I don't know who's protecting who, but you can scream if there's a problem."

She raised an eyebrow and unzipped her bag.

Eric walked over to the nearest bed and plopped down. Stretching out, he watched Simone carry some cosmetics to the bathroom. From the beginning in McGraw's Restaurant, she had been a complete mystery to him. He'd seen her as an adversary, but as of late, those impressions had been changing. She no longer seemed impossibly distant.

Giving up a woman he loved had been one of those difficult duties the spying life had demanded of him. A woman deserved a man she could count on to be there for her.

Simone hung her suit coat in the closet. Eric studied her movements.

"I'll take my bag over to my room," Eric finally said. "Think it will take long for you to get ready? Maybe we could eat at a nice restaurant tonight."

Simone smiled. "Sure."

"We can get better acquainted."

Simone laughed. "You might be taking a bigger bite than you think."

❖-❖-❖-❖

Eric followed Simone into the Queen's Quarters, an elegant restaurant across from Green Park. Propriety hung in the air like expensive perfume. Candles had already been lit.

"I believe you have a reservation for Mr. and Mrs. George Flint," Eric said to the maître d'.

"Of course." The man bowed slightly. "Please follow me."

Eric and Simone fell in behind the man. Near the rear of the restaurant, the maître d' stopped before a small table with fresh flowers in the center. "Please enjoy your meal." He placed two menus on the table and hurried away.

"A touch of refinement lends encouragement every now and then," Eric said and picked up the menu.

Simone raised an eyebrow.

"Listen, I'd hoped that this trip would give us an opportunity to become better acquainted. Maybe even become friends."

She laid the menu down. "That's probably not a good idea. Both our lives have more than a few complications."

Eric grinned. "You're a capable woman. No one could doubt your abilities. I'd like to know the person inside."

"Eric, you grew up in the security of the United States. You love those ideals that made your country great. My family comes from a different world."

"Maybe I'd like to understand a little more about that world."

Simone studied the flowers in the center of the table for a moment. "My grandparents Ari and Meira Koole lived in Warsaw, Poland. Never bothered anybody. Never hurt anyone. Just lived like their family had for hundreds of years. Then, Adolph Hitler came to town. Everything changed."

Eric nodded.

"Sensing what might be coming, my grandparents put my father on a kindertrain that wound through France. He finally ended up in London. After the war, my mother Alona was smuggled into Israel and began her life in a kibbutz. Do you have any idea how hard those times were?"

Eric shook his head. "I can only guess."

"The British hovered over our people like wolves ready to strike. The heat nearly killed them in the summer. My mother struggled to survive. On that kibbutz, she met my father, Jokin Koole. I suppose they weren't sure they could even outlast the war. Then came independence in May 1948, and Israel began again. Somehow they endured."

"And your grandparents?"

Simone stiffened. "It took some time for the final report to filter through channels and reach Israel, but eventually it did. In the Jewish ghetto in Warsaw, they joined the resistance. With meager rations and ever-depleting ammunition, they fought to the bitter end. Both Ari and Meira Silverstein died in the rubble of broken bricks and scattered glass."

Eric studied Simone's face, which showed no emotion, as if she were reporting a story told a hundred times before. He sensed that beneath that facade, her feelings plummeted and rose again like a roller coaster. Even though her facial expressions didn't change, pain lurked in the corners of her eyes.

"You have a difficult history."

Simone shrugged. "We must take what comes to us. There's no choice in the matter."

"And your father and mother?"

"My mother Alona lives some distance from Jerusalem near a little village named Zippori. She still lives in the kibbutz where my father . . ." She stopped abruptly. "She found life to be easier in the kibbutz."

"Easier?" Eric leaned across the table.

"Easier after my father was shot while he was plowing in a field." For a moment, her voice broke and then became flat again with the same emotionless emptiness it had when she described her grandparents' death. "After the murder, Alona stayed in the kibbutz."

Eric settled back in his chair and stared at her. Simone seemed to stare back without feeling. Her silent, challenging gaze left him to fill in the blanks.

"You look at me as if you almost dare me to make a response," Eric said. "As if anything I say would sound insensitive. But I know there are no words to convey how sorry I feel for what you and your family have been through."

Simone's face did not move, but a tear formed in her eye and trickled down her face. "Thank you," she said with a slight tremble in her voice. "Maybe we should order." Her eyes drifted down to the menu.

A few minutes later, the waiter approached with a small pad in hand. "What might the lady and the gentleman select this evening?"

After they placed their orders, the waiter took their menus and walked away.

Looking into Simone's eyes, Eric said, "Your journey has turned Simone Koole into a modern-day Deborah; a steadfast woman who has faced fear many times but pressed on to keep faith with her parents' and grandparents' history."

Simone's countenance cracked. Gone was her aloofness. "Thank you," she said as her voice quivered again.

"My world is, indeed, of an entirely different order. I attended Yale University and was recruited by the CIA. I grew up in Philadelphia when they instilled old-fashioned patriotism in my bloodstream, but I know nothing of what you and your family suffered."

Simone was silent a moment before speaking. "Eric, the world has not been kind to the Jews. Anyone who reads a history book knows our story of persecution. We defend ourselves while the world's journalists continue to publish anti-Israeli stories and make our political decisions sound like prejudice and hatred. We have no alternative but to maintain constant alertness. I have given my life to maintaining a wall that will keep the terrorists out of our streets and stop them from killing our children in the marketplace. Such is who I am." Simone's eyes softened. "You are a good man, Eric. I will do all that I can to preserve that quality in the world . . . and in you."

26

The St. James Hotel's doorman kept waving for a taxi. His crimson red morning coat and black top hat distinctively contrasted with the casually dressed Americans. Simone, Eric, and Dan waited at the curb, looking imported.

"Your carriage, sir." The doorman pointed to the black taxi that had just driven up.

"Thank you." Eric pressed a pound note in his palm.

"British Institute of Technology, please," Simone told the driver. "Know the way?"

"Certainly," the driver said.

The taxi surged down Pall Mall Boulevard. The three passengers said little as the taxi circled Trafalgar Square and headed west. In fifteen minutes, the vehicle slowed as they approached a large gray building.

The taxi pulled to the curb and stopped. The three travelers got out.

"I'll do the talking," Simone said.

Once inside, they took an elevator up to the fourth floor and walked to a plain door with Supervisor painted on the glass. Underneath, the name Oliver Headington had been printed in gold lettering. Simone looked up and down the hall and then entered without knocking. A tall man with gray hair sat hunched over a large desk. He blinked several times and then beamed.

"Simone, my dear!" the man said. "How good to see you."

"Oliver, you're looking well," she answered.

"A brisk walk every day keeps me in jolly good shape." Oliver winked. "I see you brought friends with you."

"Associates," Simone said. "Eric and Dan."

"Good to meet you, gentlemen." Headington came around the desk and shook their hands. Then he turned to Simone. "What can I do for you today, my dear?" He lowered his voice. "As if I didn't already know."

Simone handed him a small flash drive. "It's all in there," she said. "The program seems to be coming along nicely. We are making progress tying the units together. You'll know what to do with the rest of the assignment. We shouldn't say much about this out loud."

Headington carefully studied the device. "Hmm, I see. Rather plain, isn't it?"

"It's a challenge," Simone said. "Infecting a complex industrial system you've never seen isn't easy. Takes a great thinker like yourself to put such a system together."

"Great thinker!" Headington laughed with a touch of scorn. "Come now, my dear. You're much too generous. I must tell you this problem will take a while to solve."

"Of course," Simone said. "As always, the utmost secrecy is required."

Headington laid the flash drive on his desk. "Give me a few weeks at most," he said. "Maybe less."

"You're on." Simone smiled.

"It's a great pleasure to help the cause. Please give my highest regards to Dar Dagan when you see him next. Fine chap."

"Indeed." Simone opened the door to the office. "We'll be on our way then. Good luck."

Without pausing, the threesome walked out of the building and hailed another taxi to take them to the corner of Shepherd Market and Hyde Park. The taxi pulled up and they got out.

Simone stood on the street corner for a moment, staring out across the expansive breadth of Hyde Park. Like a hound suddenly discovering an unexpected scent in the breeze, she stood immobile, sensing some unseen entity. Finally, she turned to the men.

"Something isn't right," she said.

"Headington seemed fine to me," Eric said.

"Not him. I can't identify what's wrong, but I'm troubled."

"You get these feelings often?" Dan asked.

Simone stared at him almost with contempt but didn't answer.

"What would you suggest?" Eric asked her.

"Let's stroll across the park," Simone said. "We're tourists. Chat like old friends. Act natural but pay attention. *Careful* attention."

"Got it," Eric said.

Walking at a leisurely pace, the threesome made their way across the wide grassy area. Simone talked about once walking around the wall surrounding the ancient city of Jerusalem, and Eric described climbing Long's Peak in Colorado. Dan said little.

Simone picked up the pace. "Two men seem to have picked up our trail. I think we're being followed."

Eric reached inside his oversized shirt and unbuttoned the shoulder holster under his arm.

Simone deviated to the right, but the men followed. Fifty feet ahead, she looked around again. "They're back there. I'm sure they're following us."

"Got to play this cool," Dan said. "Keep a steady pace."

Simone nodded straight ahead. "There's a guy sitting over there in an overcoat. It's far too warm for that."

"He's got his hands in his pockets," Eric said. "We're cornered."

"Listen to me carefully," Dan said. "I'm going to drop to one knee. I want the two of you to run toward that oak tree and the bushes twenty feet to your right. Don't stop till you hit the ground. Run!"

Eric grabbed Simone's hand and jerked her forward. They raced across the grass and leaped into the shrubs. Gunfire echoed behind them; a bullet pinged overhead off the tree. Dan tumbled backward just as the man on the bench rolled off the bench and sprawled on the grass. The two assassins ran at Eric and Simone, firing automatic pistols. Rapid fire sprayed the trees.

"Hold tight!" Eric aimed his Glock. The roar of another pistol suddenly echoed in his ear.

"Got one," Simone said.

The second man stopped and then dashed for a tree on the far side of the walkway. Eric fired two shots, but both missed. The assassin broke through the thick shrubs and disappeared in the grove. The assailant fired two more shots before silence fell over the park. Eric could hear the faint sounds of a man running.

"Dan's down," Simone said.

"Police!" a voice echoed through the park. "Police!"

"Got to take care of my man, police or not." Eric stood up. "Stay here until the scene clears out. You don't need the exposure."

Eric ran across the grass and dropped beside Dan.

Dan didn't move. A bullet had hit him square in the chest.

"Dan! Can you hear me?"

Silence.

"Please! Dear God, don't let him die."

27

The police quickly cordoned off the area, stringing plastic tape around the crime scene while bobbies swarmed in from across the park. Paramedics covered Dan with a sheet and prepared to take the body to the ambulance. Eric kept his eyes fixed on Simone standing innocuously behind a crowd of watchers.

"Sorry, old man," the officer told Stone. "As best I can tell, you must have been at the wrong place at the wrong time. We've had problems with rioters and delinquent teenagers in recent days. My guess is that you stumbled into a cross fire between rival groups."

Eric nodded but said nothing.

"Don't know what to make of that chap in the topcoat lying in the grass," the officer continued. "Must have also been hit by accident."

Eric said nothing.

"Here's me card," the officer said to Eric. "You can call for information about the case."

"Thank you, officer. Can I go now?"

"Certainly."

Eric nodded and walked slowly toward the crowd. He cut through the gathering and kept walking. Simone would catch up with him when it didn't look so obvious that they were together.

For three blocks they walked apart, saying nothing. Only after they were clear of the Hyde Park area did they speak.

"Did you get his gun?" Simone asked.

"The cops questioned me but never searched me. It's stuck inside my belt."

"Good. That's why they let you off the hook and thought Dan had been caught in an unfortunate cross fire."

"Yeah." Eric slowed and looked down at the sidewalk. "Dan was more than an employee and a friend. He was like a brother."

"I understand," Simone said and lowered her head. She squeezed Eric's hand and started walking again.

They walked an entire block before Eric spoke again. "Who were the killers after? You? Me? Us?"

"I don't know," Simone said. "I can't quite see that it was me, or, as far as this trip goes, us. I thought my major adversaries had written me off as dead. You got anybody breathing down your neck?"

"I'm not sure. I'm guessing there's a few who might like to put a bullet between my ears, but I can't imagine them coming to London to try. Seems like you're a more significant target."

"I'll do some checking."

"How about touching base with the people over there in Tel Aviv?"

Simone nodded. "Let's see what they say." She stopped by a tree and pulled out her cell phone. After a long buzz, a woman's voice answered and only repeated the phone number. "This is Simone Koole. I need to speak with Dar Dagan as quickly as possible."

The phone went on hold for several minutes.

"What kind of trouble are you in now?" Dagan said.

"I just walked away from a gunfight that killed one of the Conundrum's top men. We were ambushed by three men. Any idea why?"

Silence.

"Did you hear me, Dar?"

"Yes. Yes. We have no information that any outsider is aware of the Digital Damage operation. None."

"I see," Simone said slowly.

"However, Operation Damocles in Egypt has heated up. A couple of Egyptian agents were killed last week. They've also figured out that Hamas decided you were dead too quickly. If I was going to bet on anyone coming after you today, I'd put money on the Egyptians. Hamas isn't that strong internationally."

"Makes sense. They could have picked up on me coming through passport control. A hundred different nationalities mingled together in the reception hall. I probably wouldn't have been able to notice one of their people hanging around the scene."

"I'm definitely concerned if any information has been

leaked on Digital Damage," Dar said. "I will immediately put out an alert."

"Keep me posted." Simone closed the cell phone.

"What'd your boss say?" Eric asked.

"Could be a different angle from what I thought," Simone said. "They're checking it out. Some piece of this puzzle is out of place."

28

Dan's death gnawed into the depths of Eric's being. He couldn't get the sight of him lying on the grass out of his mind. Eric tossed back and forth in bed, but sleep wouldn't come. Around 2:00, he climbed out of bed, shuffled into the bathroom, and came back with two sleeping pills. With some reluctance, he finally swallowed them.

"Can't get it off my mind," he mumbled aloud. "Dan should never have died."

Eric felt his troubled thoughts fading as the pills kicked in. A disorienting, wild ride swirled him through the endless night until blackness finally engulfed him. The pills did their job until every distraction vanished.

The next morning proved equally difficult. By the time he had showered and dressed, his head had cleared. Getting breakfast became the first order of the day. He walked to Simone's room and knocked on the door. She immediately opened it.

Eric stared. A bald-headed, rough-looking man sat in a chair on the far side of the room.

"Sit down and wait a minute," Simone said.

"*Boker tov,*" the man said.

Eric knew the Hebrew greeting and answered with the same words.

"We have much to talk about," Simone said. "Let's get to it."

"I understand you ran into trouble yesterday."

"You might say that," Simone said.

"Who's the guy?" the stranger asked, pointing at Eric.

Eric stared at the shabbily dressed man with a forlorn face. His bald head imparted a hard look. Mr. Whoever sat there chewing on an unlit cigar.

"He's fine," Simone said. "We're now Mr. and Mrs. George Flint in London on a vacation from New York City." She pointed at Eric. "Meet George."

The forlorn face silently stared back.

"George, meet Benny," Simone said.

Eric looked from Benny to Simone. "What's going on?"

"Benny flew in last night from Tel Aviv to talk with me about what happened yesterday," Simone said. "You might say Benny is a special delivery messenger."

Eric blinked several times. "Would have been nice to know he was coming."

Simone smiled but didn't answer.

"Want to talk here?" Benny said and glanced at Eric. "Or would someplace more private work better?"

"We can speak Hebrew."

Eric leaned against the chair and listened as the two spoke rapidly. Obviously, they knew each other well. After ten minutes of chatter, Simone hugged the man and said in English, "Tell the dragon man hello." Then she opened the door and ushered Benny out of the room.

Eric watched the door close behind him. "He's a Mossad agent?"

"Rather deceptive appearance, don't you think?"

"I've seen yardmen who looked more put together."

Simone grinned. "Benny Gantz is one of our finest martial arts experts as well as a hit man of considerable skill. He is worthy of the highest respect. His appearance allows him to slip in and out with little notice. Benny keeps us informed when it's important not to allow anyone to capture a telephone conversation."

"Okay. What's the update that Benny brought?"

"The attack wasn't related to our Digital Damage project. So far no leaks have been detected. Palestinian militants have been firing rockets out of Gaza at the town of Ofakim and Beersheba. One of our warplanes responded and killed a top Islamic jihad commander as well as a couple of Egyptian soldiers. For some reason, the Egyptians didn't like this. We think their response signals a split between military and political wings of Hamas. After the exchange, relations with Egypt deteriorated. Your newspapers haven't covered the situation, but it's created considerable tension between Egypt and Israel. Benny came to tell me that the attack in Hyde Park was probably sparked by this exchange. Their agents picked me up coming through Heathrow."

"You must be high on their list of targets."

"An honor." Simone smiled. "I've had a hand in several attempts to stop a few scientists who wanted to help manufacture rockets that could hit Tel Aviv. It appears that my efforts were part of the reason for the attack in the park."

Eric rubbed his chin and looked out the window. Finally,

he spoke. "So, the attack wasn't related to what we are doing here?"

"It appears not."

Eric nodded his head soberly.

"We have made arrangements to have Dan Morgan's body released from British custody. Dan will be flown back to Denver this afternoon. Please tell me what mortuary to contact. Everything else has been taken care of."

Eric caught his breath. "You've done all of that already?"

"It was the least I could do."

29

President Ebrahim Jalili knew he must treat the Supreme Leader with total and absolute respect. Ayatollah Ali Hashemi seemed to revel in the deference afforded his position, but Jalili suspected it was regard for his person that he enjoyed the most.

"You may come in now," the aide said and opened the door.

"Thank you," the president said and forced a smile. "I will follow you."

The Supreme Leader sat hunched over a desk. Without looking up, he pointed to a chair. "In a moment," he muttered.

Jalili watched him with disgust that he would never express and barely admitted to himself.

"Now," the ayatollah began, "how are we coming with the centrifuges you ordered?"

"They have arrived and are being installed even as we speak."

"And did any of our enemies identify the shipment was coming to us?" Hashemi glared through his glasses with an intensity that could burn holes in steel.

"Not to our knowledge," Jalili said with a slight hesitancy

in his voice. "The cargo landed in Syria and came by train. Of course, it is difficult to know for sure if we were observed."

"Why?" The ayatollah's voice became hard. Intimidation resounded in the one word.

"Sir, one never knows where spies lurk, but we have taken every precaution possible."

The Supreme Leader leaned back in his chair and stared at Jalili for several moments.

Jalili knew he must not reflect any emotion. Let Hashemi think what he wanted, Jalili would report only the facts. He would not in any way appear intimidated.

"I understand that the longer these centrifuges turn, the higher will be the level of enrichment and that we must reach a 90 percent level to be ready for making a bomb."

"That is correct."

"I want these machines working immediately. I want the material ready for weapon development in three months. Can you achieve this goal?"

"If this is your wish, it will be met."

"All we need is enough to drop one bomb on Tel Aviv and the world will know our power. Understood?"

"Absolutely."

❖❖❖

The United 747 hummed across the Atlantic while Eric tried to make up for lost sleep from the night before. Four hours of solid sleep helped, but he kept thinking about Dan's casket in the cargo hold of the plane.

He was flying back alone, accompanying Dan's body to Denver, while Simone flew on to Israel. On one hand, he hoped this Benny Gantz guy was right. If the shooters came from Egypt, it meant the Digital Damage project was still protected, and this took pressure off his people. Then again, Gantz's story meant Simone was in danger. He certainly didn't like that either.

George and Sarah would be at the airport with Dan's wife. Thinking about what would follow seemed almost impossible. Tears filled his eyes. The roar of the jet engines drowned out his reflections, and he drifted back to a troubled sleep.

The pilot's announcement woke him. The airplane was on final approach for Denver. Eric hustled to get ready. With only a slight bump, the plane touched down on the runway and turned toward the terminal. After a few minutes, the passengers started to exit the plane. Eric headed for the terminal tram and boarded.

Seeing Dan's wife would not be easy. Sarah and George would be distraught too. The terminal tram pulled into the final stop and emptied quickly. Eric got on the escalator that would take him to the waiting crowd.

When he reached the top, he immediately saw them standing in the crowd. Three dear, dear friends looking profoundly grieved.

⋯⋯⋯

The melancholy strains of an organ playing "Amazing Grace" imparted a solemn atmosphere that lingered over the funeral home. The chapel had been filled with Dan's friends and family. The pallbearers walked down the aisle and pulled the casket to the back door in solemn dignity. The large crowd began to disperse, but the staff of the Conundrum still sat in place, staring at the baskets of flowers lining the front of the chapel.

During the service, Eric had maintained a stoic appearance. The funeral had been handled with dignity, but Dan's loss cut to his core. He could see tears running down Bernice Morgan's face. Finally, she stood up and walked over to Eric.

"I know how much you cared about Dan," Bernice Morgan said. "Thank you for telling me how he died. Dan was always a brave man."

"Beyond measure," Eric said. "Brave to the last moment."

Bernice dabbed at her eyes. "Dan never talked about his work."

"That's true, Bernice. And Dan was always a professional. I had the utmost respect for him."

"And I always knew danger was involved. Dan didn't like me knowing he carried a gun, but he always had it handy. He wouldn't discuss the risks, but I knew in my heart of hearts that he put his life on the line." Bernice sighed. "I know you can't talk about your projects. When he was gone, I'd lie awake and worry late at night. But I always wondered what he was doing."

"Bernice, we're not just a business. We are committed to truth, to honesty, to making the world a better place. Some politicians are people of honor; some are crooks. Our job is to sort out the liars from the genuine. Dan always upheld these principles." Eric patted Bernice on the arm. "Did Dan tell you that we maintained an insurance policy on his life?"

Bernice shook her head. "No, I had no idea."

"In a couple of weeks, you'll be receiving a check for a million dollars."

Bernice's mouth dropped. She blinked several times. "A million dollars."

"We want you to be provided for, Bernice."

Bernice's eyes widened in shock. "I can't believe this."

"Dan was one of my best friends. I hope this will take care of any financial concerns you may have. If you want any advice in deciding how to invest, Sarah Fleming is an expert. She'll be glad to help you."

Bernice clutched Eric's hand and squeezed it fiercely. "God bless you, Eric. I can't begin to tell you what this means." She stood up. "Thank you. Thank you more than I can possibly say." She kissed him on the cheek before walking resolutely out of the chapel.

Eric wiped a tear from his eye.

⊰⊱⊰⊱⊰⊱

George followed Eric into his estate in the mountains above Evergreen. The two men sat down in the living room across from each other.

"Thanks for being there when we returned," Eric said. He was quiet for a moment. "I can't believe Dan's gone."

George nodded. "I know. We'll miss his wisdom in our decisions." He hung his head.

After a long silence, Eric spoke again. "While we were gone, did you make any progress on this computer assignment that Simone gave you?"

"I did. Took some fancy footwork manipulating the codes. I'm not sure why Mossad wants such a thing, but in a few more hours I believe I'll be ready to finish completing the connections."

Eric rubbed his forehead. "What would be the purpose of such a device?"

"I've given that some thought," George said. "The Syrians have always been a persistent enemy of Israel. At one point, the Israelis secretly bombed a nuclear site for fear of Syria making a nuclear bomb. They wouldn't hesitate to strike the Syrians again. Possibly this device has some part in that sort of assault. She could be aiming at their industrial capacities. Maybe trying to shut down an ammunitions facility."

"Hmm. The experts in London and Germany don't know more than we do. Right?"

George nodded his head. "We're all working in the dark."

30

Night descended over the towering mountains. Dan Morgan's funeral was behind them. One question had continued to bother Eric all afternoon, and he needed to ask. Could someone from the defunct Saddam Hussein regime still be after him? Simone's explanation that the Egyptians were behind the assault in the park made sense, but he still worried. Could an old adversary still be out there? Maybe yes; maybe no. Eric sat down at his laptop and composed an email to Simone.

The email disappeared on its way to Israel. Hopefully, Simone would pick it up soon. Leaning back in his chair, Eric wondered what she was doing right now.

❖-❖-❖

Simone had just finished a cup of coffee when her computer beeped. She set the cup down and stared at the machine in the corner of her small apartment in Tel Aviv. Benny Gantz had her email address. A couple of agents in Egypt had the same address. One contact in Iran never used the internet but had it. And Eric Stone picked up the address just before she left. Simone walked across the room and looked at her in-box. Sure enough. Eric.

For several minutes she thought about his question. Saddam Hussein's regime? Not a chance. Then again, Dar Dagan might have other ideas. She'd see.

Simone took a look in the mirror near the door. The cut on her forehead had turned into a scar. Makeup would cover some of it, but it was a new identifying mark, and that wasn't good. There wasn't anything she could do about it at the moment.

A ten-minute walk down King Saul Boulevard took her once again past the sandstone memorial to those who had given their lives for the state of Israel. As always, she paused and touched the monument. The sobering reminder brought her to a halt. She continued on to the Office, where Dagan would be waiting.

As usual, Dagan's secretary looked at her like she was some sort of intruder. "I'm not wired to blow up the building," Simone said sardonically. "You can relax."

The woman frowned. "You may go in."

Simone didn't slow her confident stride. After a brisk single knock, she opened the door and walked in. Dagan sat hunched over his desk, studying a folder from a pile of files stacked to his right. His usual open short-sleeved bland shirt looked as everyday as a slice of white bread. He adjusted his rimless glasses and looked at her with the intensity of a laser beam cutting through steel.

"Look who's here," Dagan said.

"Thanks for such a warm greeting. After all, I've been doing nothing but sitting on the beach soaking up the sun."

Dagan leaned back in his chair. "Sounds like it was a rough time in London."

"Yes. Morgan was a good man." She took a deep breath. "It appears to be open season on Simone Koole. My American contact, Eric Stone, worries that some segment of the old Saddam Hussein crowd might be shooting at him."

"Not a chance. Those boys have disappeared like the setting sun. Tell Mr. Stone not to worry. He's not that popular with them anymore. Benny Gantz's report on the Egyptians remains more to the point."

"You're certain?"

"No, Simone, I'm not." Dagan's voice became more serious and personal. "I can't tell you for a fact that the attack wasn't related to the Digital Damage project. Getting reliable intelligence out of the Muslim world has become increasingly complicated."

"They could be on to Digital Damage?"

"It's not impossible." Dagan took off his glasses and began polishing them. "There are increased terrorist attacks in southern Israel. Weakness in the Egyptian government has made their control over this area uncertain. Militants in the Hamas and Hezbollah ranks seem out of control. We've been seeing terrorist activity in the Sinai. Of course, that's a hard area for anyone to control, so the Hamas terrorists have set up shop in the area. Iranian snipers were deployed in Syria as part of Bari's crackdown and murder of his own people. We're sure Iran is shipping more soldiers in to support the Bari regime. Ten thousand Palestinian residents fled the city of Latakia when Syrian security forces descended on them. A frightening scene. No?"

"What's the story, Dar?"

"Stranger than you might think. You see, Bari's real fear is the Sunnis. His tribal background makes him an Alawite Arab, and the Syrian population is only 12 percent Alawites. The Sunnis make up 70 percent of the rest of the country. What happens if the Sunnis prevail in this uprising?" Dagan threw up his hands. "President Bari has to be terrified that the Sunnis would wipe out him and his tribesmen. He can no longer point to us as the Zionist enemy and distract the radicals. His back is to the wall."

"And what would he do if the Sunnis actually started to win?"

Dagan smiled. "He might have to turn to Israel to help him survive. How does that possible alternative grab you?"

Simone sat resolutely and stared. After a few moments of silence, she asked, "Does it look like the Arab Spring of hope may turn into a winter of despair?"

Dagan nodded his head. "Sectarian conflicts will always be with us. Iran's hunger for nuclear weapons remains a specter lurking on the horizon, waiting to descend like a vulture. We remain concerned that your work could be jeopardized."

"Where?"

"How sound is your contact in the Styman Company?"

"Otto Langer?" Simone shrugged. "I have no reason to suspect him. Do you?"

"We haven't been able to learn as much as we would like about his background." Dagan leaned back in his chair and bounced his fingertips together.

"But Langer has no idea what his work will accomplish," Simone said. "Isn't that significant?"

"Yes." Dagan nodded his head. "But he knows you. And you sent Stone to him under an alias and the man was attacked on a side street."

Simone nodded solemnly.

"You have created a network of deception. But as you know, I leave no stone unturned. I worry Otto Langer might have disclosed the names he's learned from his work with this project."

Simone took a deep breath. "I don't think roughing up the man will accomplish our goals. Perhaps tailing him, bugging his phones, hacking his computer, that sort of thing, would tell us something."

"Exactly. I've already got agents working on that. We're busy picking up everything we can find."

"In the meantime, I need Langer to finish his work," Simone said. "He's vital to the next step in our project. Don't disturb what he's doing."

"I understand, but I want you to know, we're checking him out carefully. Don't underestimate anyone. Too much is at stake."

Simone pushed her chair back and stood. "I'll stay alert." She started walking out and stopped. "I appreciate the update. Keep breathing fire."

Dagan frowned and waved his hand at her dismissively.

⋇ ⋇ ⋇

Eric awoke with a start. The cold mountain night air drifted in through his window. He blinked, and morning sunlight fell over his face. Eric turned in his bed and tried to orient himself. Some wild dream had disturbed his sleep, but he couldn't remember what it was. He pushed himself up against the headboard and tried to clear his mind.

His thoughts kept swirling around the image of Simone Koole that he carried in his mind. When she first showed up at McGraw's, he'd been so shocked that he hardly knew what to think of her. Of course, that had been exactly what she intended. The woman had proved to be a master of deception with a disconcerting ability to walk through his security systems. Her first meeting with his agents had demonstrated she was tough as nails.

But then again . . . Eric had reached through her carefully crafted facade and found a gentle, candid dimension that strongly attracted him. Simone's candor and honesty drew him more than any woman he'd met in a long time. Their worlds were different, yet strangely alike. While he couldn't identify with her background, they were both espionage agents facing danger and life-threatening circumstances every day. Both knew how costly their work could be.

Even more, Simone's fierce commitment had sprung from her faith. Clearly, she believed she was serving God. Her devotion had touched something in Eric's heart. More than he had admitted to himself, his love of his country had risen out of a personal faith deeply rooted in the Christian way. When all was said and done, Eric and Simone came through different doors but served the same God.

Here they were. Two people of different origins bent on the same task from a common source. Jew and Christian, tied together in some way that he couldn't yet grasp. Eric didn't like being in the dark, but Simone held the cards. Whether she liked it or not, they had a connection that wasn't going away.

31

Simone's car sped down the highway and across Megiddo. From Nazareth, she turned north until she came to Zippori. At the edge of town, she turned into the entrance of Kibbutz Shalom. The graveled road wound toward a large administration building and then on toward several rows of houses. Growing up in the kibbutz, she had worked in the nearby fields and knew the area well. Kibbutz Shalom had started a plywood business and had done well. The shanties that her parents had once lived in had been replaced by nice bungalows with brick fronts connected by winding paths bordered by flower beds bright with red, gold, and blue flowers.

Returning home always left Simone with conflicted feelings. Life had never been easy, although she was well fed and loved. She grew up surrounded by a multitude of "aunts" and "uncles" who cared for her. The men often tousled her long black hair and the women gave her kisses and hugs. Simone never lacked the warmth of friends who treated her like a member of a large family. At the same time, tragedy had never been a stranger to the kibbutz. Virtually everyone had either survived a death camp or was a descendant of survivors. Attacks by terrorists were always possible. During the Yom Kippur and the Six-Day wars, many of the men died. Her own father had died in these fields.

Simone tried unsuccessfully to block the memory of the day shots rang out across the kibbutz. Men and women ran. Screams echoed from the fields. Panic seized the kibbutz, and people dove under benches and outdoor tables. Little Simone had stood frozen on the grass.

"Jokin Koole's been hit!" rang through the air. "Someone help Jokin! Help us! Help us!"

Little Simone started to run to the field. From out of nowhere, a hand grabbed her and dragged her to the ground.

"Stay down!" the man's voice demanded. "They'll shoot you!"

She tried to wrestle away, but he held her pinned to the ground. "They'll kill anyone," he whispered in her ear. "You mean nothing to them."

Simone still tried to get up, but she couldn't. Eventually the shooting stopped. When the man let go, she recognized Harel Skaat, a man who worked in the plywood factory. He pulled her toward the wooden administration building and pushed her inside.

"Stay in here," Harel warned. "Make sure all is clear before you go out. Understand?" he said harshly.

Simone could only nod her head.

Thirty minutes passed before they brought Jokin out of the field on a stretcher. Someone had wrapped a heavy bandage around his head, but it was already soaked in blood. His arm dangled lifelessly from the side of the stretcher. She saw her mother, Alona, running from their small wooden house, screaming at the top of her voice, "Jokin! God help us! Oh, Jokin!"

Men set the stretcher down while someone backed a pickup near where he lay on the grass to take him to the hospital. Alona fell over his limp body, sobbing bitterly. Her father never moved.

On this sunny afternoon, Simone stared at the same spot on the grass where her father had once lay. Today, it seemed peaceful and quiet. Tears began running down her cheeks. For a long time she stood there weeping.

Finally, Simone turned toward her mother's housing unit. As always, she knocked. A small woman with gray hair opened the door. "Simone!"

"Boker tov!" Simone hugged her mother. "I've come for a little visit."

"My dear, dear child!" She threw her arms around her neck. "What a wonderful surprise. Come in and sit down."

The passing years had made her mother more frail, but she knew that Alona would maintain her endurance no matter what. The two of them still looked a great deal alike, although her mother's face had become thinner and more drawn. Simone knew her mother had never completely recovered from her husband's death, but she seldom spoke of it these days.

"I must fix you a little coffee." Alona shuffled off to the kitchen. "Sit down in here and tell me what you are doing these days."

"Mama, I really can't talk about what I do, but I'm working for Israel and our people. I always will."

"Yes, I know," Alona said quietly. "I assume you are in danger?"

"Don't worry about such things. I play a small role in the larger system. No one's interested in me."

Alona stopped and looked intensely at her daughter. "We have both lived too close to the edge to pretend with one another. I pray for you each day."

"Knowing you care encourages me more than I can possibly say."

Alona set a cup of coffee in front of Simone and sat down across from her. "Our people have not had an easy time of it. Even in Europe, hate has started to work again. We always get the raw end of the deal when the media reports on what we are doing. Even now we are surrounded by countries that want to destroy us."

"Don't worry, Mama. Our problems are not going unnoticed." Simone reached across the table and took her mother's hand. "Trust me. Regardless of how the winds blow, we *are* confronting our opponents."

32

Simone closed the door to her mother's home and walked slowly toward her car. She was unable to come often and missed the orderly quietness of Kibbutz Shalom. The smell of freshly turned dirt filled her nose. Security was much improved around the farm, and people no longer feared for their lives. The deaths of people like her father had been a high price for their current safety.

"What is this that I see?" an old voice said from somewhere behind her.

Simone turned to see who was speaking.

"I swear that this grown woman looks remarkably like our Little Miss Bright Eyes," the voice continued. "Amazing resemblance."

Simone looked behind her. An old man with a long flowing beard and a broad smile sat hunched over on a dilapidated outdoor bench under a large tree. The worn black yarmulke perched on his head made a sharp contrast with the bright white hair hanging down into his eyes. He had to be in his nineties. Sitting with his hands folded over his protruding stomach, he looked like an antique from a bygone era.

"Rabbi Cohen!" Simone rushed toward the bench. "I know

you don't even shake hands with a woman to avoid all ap-
pearances of temptation, but I am going to kiss your forehead
anyway." She bent down and kissed him. "I have missed you
terribly."

"Ah, my tired old eyes did not deceive me. Bless you, my
child. Little Miss Bright Eyes has returned. You have come
back to our kibbutz."

"Kibbutz Shalom will always be my home. I'm afraid I
don't get back often."

"And you still work for Mossad?"

"Every day."

"You keep us safe."

"We try."

"Excellent. Here, sit down beside me."

Simone sat down. "How is your health?"

"I am so old that I should have died long ago, but I keep
on puttering along. Who knows when I will die? Maybe any
day now."

"Your wife, Tova." Simone hesitated. "She . . . is . . ."

"Gone," the rabbi said. "Tova died a decade ago, and every
day I miss her. We buried her close to your father's grave. I
don't know how I have lived without her. But we have no
choice, do we? We must go on." The rabbi sighed. "And you?
Have you found a nice Jewish boy for a husband?"

"I'm too busy. Chasing the bad guys doesn't leave much
time for romance."

The rabbi studied her face. "But you travel out of the country. You spend time in the world of the goyim. These outsiders
have shown no interest in this beautiful face?"

Simone didn't answer.

"You must be cautious, my child. Remember the stories in the Torah." The rabbi shook his finger. "They serve as a guide for you, instruction that will keep you pure."

"What do you mean, Rabbi?"

"Remember the story of Jacob? His mother Rebekah said to his father Isaac that she had become sick of life because the Hittite women, the daughters of the land, pursued Jacob. Isaac warned his son Jacob that he must not take a wife from among the Canaanite women. He advised his son to travel to Paddan-aram and find the house of Bethuel, the family of his own blood. There among his own people, Jacob would find a wife who would help him carry the covenant forward. Remember the story?"

"Of course I do."

"The Torah says, 'Jacob left Beersheba' when it only needs to tell us that he went to Haran. The rabbis teach that with the departure of a righteous man, a tzaddik, an aura of light departs with him. The eleventh-century rabbi Rashi said that when the light departs, the honor of the city has also departed. Do you see how important a tzaddik is? You must always seek such a man as Jacob for a husband."

The rabbi grinned. "You are a special girl. You grew up among us like a lily of the field. You must not waste yourself on some outsider to the House of Israel. Rebekah was right to worry that a Hittite woman might lure Jacob away from the journey the Holy One, blessed be he, had for him. The children of Israel have a destiny, and you are one of them. *HaShem* has plans for you, and you must never forget that."

Simone raised an eyebrow. "I wasn't planning to stand under a canopy with some foreign stranger."

"Good," the rabbi said. "Very good. We will keep a canopy reserved. You must also remember what became of Jacob's brother Esau. This man had no interest in the covenant, and he wandered off after the women from the land around them. Esau went to Ishmael, Abraham's son from Hagar, and took a wife named Mahalath. The Torah tells us that Esau added wickedness upon his wickedness. Because he violated the demand to stay among his people, evil followed. Our people have been preserved through the centuries because we took the necessity of separation seriously. You must not overlook this principle. Every time you light the candles as a Sabbath begins, you must remember this principle. Can you promise me you will not forget?"

Simone nodded her head slowly. "How can I ever forget where I came from, my family, Kibbutz Shalom? I will always remember, but right now I am not looking for a nice Jewish boy to settle down with. Every day, I work for the protection of our people."

"Your father would be pleased to hear those words, Simone."

She stood up and smiled at the rabbi. She waved a final good-bye. "Shalom, my friend."

33

The drive around Nazareth and through Afula wound through the mountains and hill country. Spiked with small rocks and stones, the vacant field appeared as if pebbles were the main crop. Red poppies swayed in the gentle breeze. Simone passed Megiddo, driving south toward Tel Aviv.

At 10:00 a.m., her car radio reported the news that Syria's Bari had ordered his troops, backed by hundreds of tanks, to descend on the city of Hama. Resistance had been going on there for a week with heavy assaults from Syrian troops. In spite of international condemnation, Bari had not backed down from his bloody attacks in the area. Six Arab Gulf nations had urged Syria to reconsider, but nothing slowed the assault. Human rights activists estimated that over two hundred Syrians had been killed. The United States and European countries were considering new sanctions against Syria even though nothing slowed their aggression.

Simone zoomed past the cutoff to Umm al-Fahm and thought about the report. The Syrians wouldn't like the negative PR and the veiled threats, but such things never slowed Zefah Bari, the father, and the same would be true for the son.

The United States might press sanctions against Syrian banks and businesses that facilitated the government's illicit activities, but no one would do more. The attacks would continue.

She knew Lebanese troops had opened fire on Israeli soldiers working on their own side of the Blue Line drawn up by the United Nations. An Israeli Defense Force patrol working near Dan Kibbutz in the far north had been fired on and in turn fired back. Israel's president had already declared that the Israeli soldiers acted as necessary with every right to protect themselves. But the point remained clear: the entire region had started to boil. Any city might explode at any time. The reports coming in from Iran indicated they were going full speed ahead in the development of a nuclear device. The dragon man's best reports indicated their centrifuges were spinning full tilt.

She had told her mother the truth. No problem went unnoticed, and their opponents would be confronted, but it didn't make their nation any less vulnerable. Alona understood the exposure and the imminent danger it imposed. Then again, she had lived under such conditions and accepted the chaos as part of the price they paid for living in Israel.

❖·❖·❖

Dar Dagan walked into Simone's office with his usual fast-paced gait and a hard, determined look on his face that meant he allowed no nonsense. He perched across from her like a rooster claiming the entire barnyard.

"We've been working on your issues for several weeks. Investigating Otto Langer in particular. To this point, we've not turned up one problem."

Simone said nothing.

"We don't see any reason to distrust him *yet*. That situation may change, but you can continue working with him for now. You know we squeeze every drop of information out of a subject. I'm sure Langer is okay, but we'll keep an eye on him for a while."

Simone nodded.

"We continue to believe the attack in England was retaliation by the Egyptians for the killing of German rocket scientists in their country. We have no evidence to the contrary."

"Got ya. I'm on my way outta here."

"Go via Stuttgart on your way back to the United States. We see no reason not to pick up what Langer's been working on."

"And if you're wrong, you'll ship my body back to Israel. Right?"

"We're not hiding anything from you, Simone. Langer looks okay."

Simone took a deep breath. "Look, Dar. I saw my mother yesterday. She's lived through many tragedies, including the death of my father. She knows how to face horrid situations, but my death would kill her. Would you keep that in mind?"

Dagan leaned back in the chair for the first time. The harshness drained out of his eyes and his face sagged. He took his glasses off and rubbed his eyes. "My dear, I understand. I trust we will not have to deal with such an issue." He put his glasses back on. "But . . . if some unexpected situation arises . . . I will personally drive to Zippori to deliver the news myself."

"Thank you, Dar. I appreciate it."

34

The flight from Tel Aviv landed in Stuttgart, Germany, on time. Grabbing a taxi outside the terminal, Simone quickly found her way to Freundin Pub. The *hofbräuhaus* always bustled with tourists and locals, and she knew it was a good place to make contact. Inside the noisy bar, Simone spotted Otto Langer sitting by himself at the back. She waved. Langer immediately motioned for her to join him. Simone hurried through the crowded room.

"*Mein liebe!*" Langer grasped her hands. "How wonderful to see you again."

Simone felt him squeeze her right hand and slip a small plastic object into her palm.

"You look as beautiful as always."

"Ah, Otto. You are such a sly fox." She dropped the flash drive into her pocket.

"I must be, in a world like ours." Langer frowned. "Sit down and have some coffee with me."

"I can't stay long. I have to catch a flight this evening."

"I understand. Is your work going well?"

"Otto, the real question is about *your* work. Has it been succeeding?"

"Well." He stopped and grinned. "I think you will be pleased. My project has gone better than I would have imagined. I had to switch several codes and work some magic on the program, but I believe everything is in order. You should have no problems."

Simone reached across the table and squeezed his hand. "Excellent. You have no idea what good news this is."

Langer winked. "We all have our deadlines, and I know how important they can be. I am hopeful we have enabled you to continue on schedule."

"Definitely. Most definitely."

"When will I know if we have been successful?"

Simone shrugged. "Perhaps never. But if you read the newspapers carefully, I think you might be able to figure something out in the not-too-distant future."

"I understand," Otto said. "Such is the business we are in."

Simone patted his hand. "Possibly, on another day, I will have the opportunity to explain all the details."

"It is not necessary, my dear. If I have been able to play a small part, then I am a happy man. God bless you in your trip home. I pray for your safety."

Simone hesitated a moment. "Might I ask you a personal question? I know your birth family placed you with the Langers to escape the Holocaust. It must have been quite a shock to discover that your original name had been Meir Goldman."

Otto Langer's eyes became hazy and he stared at her with a distant expression. Slowly, he seemed to bring her back into focus. "When you discover your true identity is not what you always believed, the experience is overwhelming."

"How did you find out?"

"No one told me. One weekend I came back from the Institute of Science in Heidelberg and sat down at my father's desk to study. I noticed a few books had been pulled off a shelf and at the back a small door had been left open. My father kept a hidden wall safe, and inside were letters and documents. Out of curiosity, I started reading the letters."

Simone laughed. "You have always been a man of great curiosity."

"I found one letter that took my breath away. My mother's sister had written that they had taken in a child named Meir, but that his family had not escaped. No one knew what had happened, but my mother believed they were executed. My mother's sister wanted the Langers to take this child and rename him Otto. I was shocked out of my mind."

"Of course."

"My new family feared Hitler and his regime. They had no illusions about what the Nazis were capable of doing. Following the collapse of the Third Reich, the Allies imposed a de-nazification program on all the schools. I grew up with awful pictures of death camps and knowing what the Reich had done. Of course, on Sunday we attended church. I quickly learned that no one had ever been a Nazi or approved of the party. Lies, of course. But people didn't want to admit their enthusiastic support of Hitler. They simply wanted to survive and have something to eat at night."

Simone nodded. "Then Otto Langer found out he was Meir Goldman?"

"I had seen pictures of Jewish bodies stacked like firewood. Never would I have dreamed I could have been one of them. Those scenes burned a profound awareness in my mind." Langer shook his head. "I obviously couldn't tell my parents about my feelings."

"Did they ever intend to tell you about your past?" Simone asked. "Your history?"

"No." Otto shrugged. "They never did. But I could never be critical of them. The Langers were loving people who firmly believed in Jesus and tried to live by his teachings."

"Good. I am glad to hear that."

"You know the rest of my story. When I realized that I could be of help to Israel, I had a burning passion to do so. My work with computers has proven to be of value. I have been delighted."

"So, you have lived with one foot in both worlds ever since?"

"Strange, isn't it? But I have found that I could worship in either a synagogue or a church. Both groups have important differences, but I stay away from arguments. I cannot deny how I was raised, but I know in my soul that I was born a Jew and when I die, I will die a Jew. I have made arrangements to be buried in a Jewish cemetery."

"Your story encourages me, Otto. I know a man who is a Christian." Simone's words seeped out slowly and thoughtfully. "He stands committed to truth and justice. I believe him to be a good man."

Otto chuckled. "I see a twinkle in your eye, my dear. Many of our women have married such men. I know intermarriage is forbidden among the Orthodox, but I never lived in their world. I cannot find a problem with such a person."

"Interesting."

"Judaism has always carried a broad range of opinions. You already know that in Israel the majority of the population does not agree with the austere people who live *Mea She'arim* and practice a rigid faith. Is that not so?"

"Yes. You are correct."

"You know the old saying, 'two Jews; three opinions.' If you believe such is true, how can you turn your back on a relationship with a good Gentile?"

Otto Langer struck a nerve that Rabbi Cohen had touched earlier. She could not respond, but neither could she ignore the struggle.

Simone smiled. "Thank you." She slid out of the booth. "We serve a great cause. *Baruch atah!*" Simone hurried out of the pub and hailed a taxi. In seconds, she was on her way back to the airport.

Only after she had cleared security and boarded the flight for London did she allow herself to reach into her pocket and study the small computer memory device. The three-inch storage device looked like any other data saver. But from what Otto had said, it wasn't. She didn't understand the technical details, but she trusted her friend. The first piece of the puzzle stood ready to be slipped into service. If the rest of the trip went this well, they would be ready to strike.

⊰⊱ ⊰⊱ ⊰⊱

Simone had dozed as the Airbus flew over Europe and awoke as it was landing at Heathrow Airport. Getting through passport control always took time, but she expected it. Not much was left of the day, so she had to hustle to get to the British Museum.

As had been planned, Simone strolled through the galleries slowly as if inspecting treasures from the past. Finally, she descended to the Ancient Egypt Gallery in the basement where the famous black Rosetta Stone stood. For a few moments, she walked around the large hunk of rock with hieroglyphics on top and Greek beneath where Egyptian symbols were translated into Greek syntax. The finding of this one piece of work had broken open the ancient vernacular of the first civilization that made pyramids.

"You will notice how deeply the two languages have been carved into the rock," a man said behind her.

Simone turned to find Oliver Headington pointing at the large rock.

"Quite a discovery," Headington said. "Amazing how such finds reshape history." He took hold of her arm and pulled her to one side. "Look at it from this angle." His hand slid down her sleeve.

Simone felt something small drop into her pocket.

"Discovery is everything," Oliver said. "Amazing what research can produce."

"And has it worked for you?"

Headington smiled. "Indeed! I think everything is in order."

"Good. Then, my visit to the museum has proven valuable. I cannot fully express our appreciation to you."

"My pleasure."

Simone stopped and looked him in the eye. "Bless you."

Oliver Headington simply nodded his head and walked away.

35

The flight from London via Newark landed in Denver International Airport at 10:00 a.m. Still feeling groggy, Simone knew a nice long shower would put vitality back into her step. Walking through the crowded corridors with affluent tourists in their flip-flops and T-shirts that promoted football teams felt foreign to the world she had just left. The international scene with its wide diversity of clothing, head coverings, skin colors, and clashing colors had evaporated, leaving only Bermuda shorts, cowboy hats, and boots. She hurried out of the airport.

"Taxi!" Simone waved from the cement driveway. "Taxi!" A yellow cab pulled up, and she hopped in.

"Going to Aurora. I need to take Ward Street off of I-70."

The driver nodded and drove away. Leaning against the backseat, Simone once again thought about Eric Stone. He was somewhat older, but she liked older men because they had maturity and focus. She had not allowed herself to think about what a handsome man he was. Actually, Eric seemed oblivious to his appearance. Had he noticed her? Simone couldn't tell. Maybe he had. Hopefully, he had.

Over the years as the assignments piled up in the Office, she had forced herself to keep her mind off men. Mossad agents had approached her, but she purposefully gave off "not interested" vibes.

The taxi rolled down the busy interstate highway, crossing downtown Denver in record time and finally turning up Ward Street. When the driver pulled in front of the old apartment building, she paid him and hurried inside.

A hot shower was the first order of business. After standing longer than usual in the hot water, Simone finally stepped out and began drying her hair. The warm air felt renewing and refreshing. Wrapping a large towel around her body, she shut off the dryer and opened the bathroom door.

"Hello, Ms. Koole."

Simone bolted back against the wooden door.

"Welcome back to Colorado," Sarah Fleming said.

"How did you get in here?"

"You underestimate the Conundrum organization, Simone. We're not quite the clods you think we are."

"How'd you find this apartment?"

"We, too, know how to show up unannounced." Sarah's tan knit leggings, riding boots, and a matching tan weave top had her usual *très chic* look. "Nice place."

Sarah knew how to play the game as well as Simone did.

"What is it you want?" Simone said.

"I've come to take you to our offices. Thought you might appreciate a ride."

"I have a car," Simone said. "I can get myself there without an escort."

"Good. Then I'll wait out front and follow you." Sarah sauntered out of the room. The game had definitely gotten more complicated.

36

Simone felt outmaneuvered, and she knew the entire staff would have heard the story. She'd been given a reminder that they knew how to play hardball.

"Ah, Ms. Koole," George Powers said. "Good to see you. I trust you have the memory devices from Europe that I need to work on."

Simone nodded.

"Ah, good." George smiled broadly, and his magnified eyes rolled behind his Coke-bottle glasses.

Simone reached into her purse and produced the memory devices she had picked up in Stuttgart and London.

"Your assignment is to merge these two programs into one unit, George. The basic work has already been done. You need to include their programming into what you've been working on. Think you can do it?"

George picked up the two small USB storage devices. "I'll give it a try."

"More than a try." Simone's voice hardened. "We need it quickly."

"Yes, of course." George turned back to his desk and began tapping away on his computer keyboard.

Out of the corner of her eye, Simone saw Sarah slip in through the door and then retreat.

❖ ❖ ❖

Around 4:00 in the afternoon, George called Simone in to his workshop. "I found joining these components much easier than creating one." He pointed to his computer screen. "Of course, I won't know for sure that it works until you tell me what we're doing so that I can make a test. Do I qualify for confidential information yet?"

Simone paused. "Let's see if we can find out if this little creation clicks." She walked around the office slowly, considering several approaches that might test the device's capacity without disclosing the actual intent. George sat patiently twiddling his thumbs. She glanced at the clock. George said nothing.

Simone snapped her fingers. "George, can you keep that program open on one screen while we look at a website on another?"

"Certainly."

"Al-Qaeda's produced a website that grinds out their propaganda. Rather annoying to listen to. Perhaps we can put a cork in their bottle. Let's see what our little program can do."

George began typing. The website came up. He leaned back in his chair and watched images and Arabic script pop up on the monitor.

"Okay. I want you to target this website with our new program so that our instructions can filter in."

"Hmm." George twisted his mouth and rubbed his chin. "That's a little more complicated than it sounds. We'll have to penetrate a firewall to get there."

He leaned over the screen and began typing. For the next forty-five minutes, Simone sat silently watching.

"I think I'm into their website," George mumbled softly. "Yes, it looks like I'm in."

"Excellent." Simone jumped out of her chair. "Let's see." She peered over his shoulder.

"What next? Want to slip into their email and gum up the works?"

"No. Let's do something a tad more destructive."

"Like what?"

"If our little present works, it will destroy the website so it won't function again."

George rubbed his chin. "Let's see what happens." He began typing.

Simone studied the monitor. Thirty seconds after George typed in his message, the screen went blank.

"Got it!" George shouted.

Simone studied the empty screen. Every bit of al-Qaeda's hogwash had evaporated. Their coded instructions had destroyed the site so effectively, it would probably never come back in that form. At least, that was her intent.

"Thank you, George. You have no idea how important this milestone is."

"Now I know what I need to finish the project. I'll add a component that will allow you to get in without taking the route I did on my computer. I'll put in the codes, and you'll be ready to strike."

"You're a genius, George. I can't express how much I appreciate what you've done."

Simone walked out. She felt like some of the burden she carried had lifted.

"Got a moment?"

Simone looked through the door. Sarah Fleming had her riding boots propped up on a chair.

"I'd like a word with you."

Simone studied the woman carefully. The smugness had gone and she seemed more conciliatory. "Sure."

"Close the door, please." Sarah waited for Simone to sit down. "I know I startled you this morning. Sorry."

"You're the first person to drop in on me at that address, and you certainly caught me in an unexpected moment."

Sarah smiled. "Look, Simone. Around here, we don't treat each other like logs for the fire. Of course, we have our little squabbles and disagreements. I beat on George and he beats on me. Underneath all that, we care about each other. The Conundrum has become more like a family. You'll get a lot more out of us if you'll relax and treat us like we're members of your tribe."

Simone studied Sarah's eyes. No guile. No deception. The woman meant what she said.

"I hear you, Sarah."

"We're here because we believe in a cause. We're better when we work together than when we go it alone. Make sense?"

For the first time in years, Simone felt her guard slip, but that seemed okay. Sarah had offered a hand, and she needed to take it. It meant relinquishing her games of superiority over the organization. "Yes, I understand what you're saying."

"I'm as competitive as they come. Don't like to lose. But, that's mainly for outsiders. Simone, why don't you come on inside with us and be one of our gang?"

Simone looked at the floor. The woman came from a totally different world than she did, but Sarah Fleming had just suggested a better way for her to operate. Maybe, just maybe, working together would be more productive.

"I appreciate what you're saying. Okay. We're all on the same team." Simone extended her hand.

"Good." Sarah reached across the desk. "Consider me your friend."

37

"Got a minute? I think I've got something." George shut Eric's office door behind him.

Eric closed the file he was reading. "I knew you would."

"I still don't know exactly what this Digital Damage project targets, but after analyzing the memory devices she's given me, I have determined they're designed to tie into industrial systems. I can only guess what the program might accomplish, but it has highly significant destructive capacities."

"Destructive capacities?'"

George rolled his eyes. "Well . . . I'd say we've created what amounts to malware . . . programs designed to attack other systems with directives that wipe them out."

"You did something like that with Simone's device?"

"Yeah. Blew an al-Qaeda propaganda site into cyber outer space."

"Nice work."

George shrugged. "I still don't know what the woman's after. Our little trick of slipping Sarah into Simone's apartment seems to have taken her down a notch or two. I believe she may treat us like partners rather than lackeys."

Eric smiled. "Maybe change is in the air."

"Here's the bottom line, Eric. We've created a 'worm' for electronic warfare. I'm not sure how they did it, but the Israelis found a hole in the computer system of one of their adversaries and they are prepared to hit the bad boys big-time."

Eric inhaled deeply. "Fascinating."

"The work is more sophisticated than any computer program I've ever seen. Whoever these analysts in Europe were, he, she, or they knew the world of electronics inside out. What this hacker crew came up with is absolutely genius."

"I'm not surprised at the quality of the work," Eric said. "But I wish we knew where this project was going."

"I don't think we're going to get it anywhere but from Simone. She's the key to the entire works."

Eric leaned back in his chair and stared at the ceiling. "I'll talk to her," he finally said.

⬦⬦⬦

The sun slowly set while the moon began to drift over the mountains. The usual brisk night breeze spread a chill across Evergreen. Simone sat on the veranda and watched the shadows fall over the meadow.

"Would you like to drive down and watch the ducks on Evergreen Lake?" Eric asked. "It's a peaceful sight. Makes a nice change of pace."

"I love that lake. The lush greens and blues blend like a watercolor painting," Simone said. "The water always makes me feel peaceful. There's hardly a ripple this time of day."

"You've been there already?"

"Yeah, I stop occasionally when coming up here."

Eric extended his hand. "My car's sitting below. Ready to go?"

Simone took his hand and he pulled her up from the chair. For a moment, she felt the warmth of his palm. Strength seemed to gently flow from his touch.

"I often park down by the lake house even in winter," Eric said. "By Christmas, the ice gets so thick that the surface becomes a hockey and skating rink. It's quite a switch to see our local bay in the summer and then come back in the winter when it turns into a winter wonderland."

Simone smiled. "We don't do those sports in Israel. Never get enough ice. Mount Hermon accommodates skiing in the winter, but I'm afraid the Dead Sea always has the heater on."

Eric shut the car door behind her. The vehicle wound down the mountain until they came to the serene lake. He pulled into the empty parking area and turned off the engine.

"Gorgeous this time of the evening," Eric said.

"Yeah."

"Simone, I know you can't be happy about the surprise Sarah gave you this morning."

"How'd you find me?"

"We know Denver like the back of our hands, and the suburb of Arvada is easiest for us to access. We have our own checkpoints if we need to know who's coming and going. The airport. Bus stations. Public transportation. Actually, George hacked into the airline roster and discovered when you'd arrive. We followed you to Ward Street."

Simone shook her head. "Clever, Eric. Simple but clever. The straightforward procedures always turn out to be the most effective."

"None of us can avoid making mistakes somewhere along the way. That's why the Conundrum works like a team. We cover each others' backs. Like Dan did for us."

"I get the point." Simone looked thoughtfully out over the adjacent golf course. "You and your team are the products of democracy. You value working together." She paused. "I guess the bottom line is that I can learn something from you."

Eric smiled. "We learn from each other. We trust each other."

"Trust is an interesting word," Simone said. "When you've had friends and family killed for no other reason than hate, it's hard not to keep looking over your shoulder every minute."

Eric was silent a moment. "Not one of us takes your struggles lightly. Let us inside that part of your life, and we'll walk with you."

Tears filled the corners of Simone's eyes. "I just don't talk about my struggles often." She took a deep breath. "I don't know if I ever can." Tears trickled down her cheeks.

Eric pulled her close. Her body trembled against his chest, and tears flooded over his shirt. He hugged her even more tightly. They clung to each other while darkness settled over them. Finally, Simone straightened. Eric studied her damp eyes reflecting moonlight and then kissed her gently. She hesitated, then returned the kiss. Once again, they clung to each other in the dim of the evening.

Then Simone pushed him away. "I don't know how this happened," she said. "I let my guard down twice today, apparently."

"This isn't something I do either."

"We can't let this go any further, Eric. My life is already

given for the destiny of Israel. I'm prepared to die for my faith and my people. And it could happen at any time."

Eric nodded. "Again, me too. I've stayed away from relationships for the same reasons. I know what it is to face death every day. Dan's death was a painful reminder."

Simone wiped her eyes. "Yes. Yes."

Eric smiled. "Looks like the cards are stacked against us."

Simone abruptly smiled. "I know. But if we are destined to live on the edge, then maybe I should just take your hand and jump over the cliff with you."

Eric studied her face before reaching over and wiping a tear from her cheek. "You mean it?"

Simone put her hand on his cheek and nodded her head.

Eric pulled her closer again. "I think I could like this."

Simone smiled. "I think so too."

38

Simone watched Eric's team assemble around the conference table. A day had passed since Sarah had invaded her apartment, and Simone knew it was important to handle this meeting in a positive way. George smiled and winked, offering her reassurance. Eric followed him into the room.

"I called this meeting today because I want to thank each of you," Simone began. "The initial phase of Digital Damage has been completed because of your hard and diligent efforts. George's success with the USB storage devices has placed us in a remarkable position. I personally thank each of you for how you helped.

"I know that you've wondered why I've been silent about this device's use. I'm sure you've concluded that I didn't trust you." Simone stopped and took a deep breath. "Well—that's not untrue. When I arrived, I was leery. I didn't know you and wasn't sure of your intentions. Time has proved me wrong. I now know you care as deeply about your work as I do mine. I apologize."

The group nodded and smiled.

"I know you still have questions. What have we been

building and what will it be used for and to accomplish what end? I'm sorry that I cannot give you that information. It's not because I don't trust you, but I must defer to the decisions made by my superiors in such matters. But I want you to know that what you've built will have a great bearing on world peace."

"There is another phase?" Sarah asked.

"The next part of my task will happen outside the United States. I may still need you to help me, but I'll be on my own. I know your best wishes go with me."

George kept smiling. "We'll be waiting to help if you need us."

"Thank you, George. Your support means more than I can express. Tomorrow morning I'll be on my way out of the country." She looked around the group slowly. Her eyes stopped on Eric. "I will miss you." She looked down. "Thank you for everything."

Sarah walked toward the door but paused to pat Simone on the back as she passed by. George stopped and squeezed her hand.

Simone looked at the other end of the table. Eric sat there staring at her, saying nothing. She had learned to watch his eyes and lips. His eyes always had a telling expression when he was moved emotionally; his mouth became firm when he was worried. Simone could see clearly that Eric had been troubled by what she said. He didn't move. She kept her eyes riveted on him.

"Simone, this device will obviously be used inside a hostile country. It's designed to attack industrial networks. Am I correct so far?"

Simone nodded her head. "Yes."

"And you're going into a country where you'll stand out as a woman alone. While you are dark complexioned, you don't look like an Arab. The bottom line is clear. Your chances of surviving this assignment are poor."

"All our assignments are dangerous. I have no other alternative."

He leaned forward. "Yes, you do."

Simone knew he was up to something. "And what is that?"

"I'm going with you."

"What?"

"Hear me out. We've worked together since that day in McGraw's Restaurant. We haven't always been friends, but we've been through a lot together. In the last twenty-four hours, we've gone from being colleagues to being more than just that."

Simone wanted to retreat. She'd come to care about him too much. Obviously, he felt the same way. How could they work together under such circumstances?

"I know what you're thinking," Eric pushed. "You're afraid our relationship will get in the way. Wrong. Who would be better at covering your back than someone who cares about you? Last night you said we could join hands and go over the cliff together. I'm not saying that we're about to jump, but we are walking up to the edge." He held out his arm. "Will you take my hand?"

"Eric, I have superiors I must answer to."

"True, but from day one, you've been in charge of this operation. But you don't have to go it alone. We're going on this ride together."

"But what will Dar Dagan say—"

"He knows who I am. I'm sure he knows my personal history. You don't have anyone in Mossad better qualified than I am to cover your back. I'm going with you whether you like it or not."

"Eric, you don't realize where I'm going. You'd be in as great a danger as I am."

"I've spent my life wandering in and out of dangerous places. Don't give me lame excuses."

Normally she would have vetoed his offer in an instant, but she could tell Eric wasn't buying it. He wouldn't back off. Period.

"How soon do you want me to be ready to leave?" he asked.

"I fly out tomorrow morning."

"I'll be ready." He stood up and walked around the table. He started toward the door and stopped. "Don't worry. We'll work fine together." He bent over and kissed her. "We normally don't kiss each other around here." He winked and walked out.

Simone sat glued to her chair. She couldn't move. Why had she kissed him last night? No matter how much she argued, Simone knew she couldn't keep Eric from getting on the airplane with her. Eric had been right about one thing—her back would be covered.

⋄⋄⋄

George Powers let Eric out at the curb of Denver International Airport. He grabbed his bag out of the backseat and waved good-bye.

"Thanks, George. I'll let you know when we land."

"Take care of yourself and keep your pistol handy out there in Wherever-You-Are-Going Land."

Eric walked into the terminal and checked his bag. He found Simone outside the security area. Dressed in jeans and a sweatshirt with Harvard stenciled across the front, she looked younger than usual. Just another typical tourist.

The security check took the usual twenty minutes. Then the two-story escalator moved them up to the international area. When they reached their gate, Eric pointed to the sign over the counter.

"Is London our final destination?"

"No. That's where we get our next instructions."

39

The bright noon sun beamed into Tehran's presidential offices of Ebrahim Jalili. His five major advisers sat across from him, watching as he finished reading the document on his desk. Jalili closed the pages and pushed them into a folder marked Top Secret.

Majid Samed had come in from Shahid Beheshti University, where he worked on nuclear research, while Fereydon Zara was a longtime member of the Revolutionary Guard. Aban Tamir had recently been promoted to head Iran's atomic energy program. Both Ferran Tarif and Zafir Sabih were career politicians who had risen to the top with the election of Jalili.

"Gentlemen," President Jalili began, "we have accomplished an amazing feat. This report from the Fordow facility near Qom confirms that we now have nearly a thousand centrifuges running at full capacity. In a short time, we will have a 90 percent enriched amount of nuclear material that we can stockpile. I don't have to tell you what this means."

Fereydon Zara grinned. "The Revolutionary Guard will

rejoice. We have long waited for the capacity to stand toe-to-toe with the world's nuclear powers and force them to retreat. Our brothers will understand that this is no small achievement."

"Of course, you are being informed because of the positions that you hold. No one must know that we have acquired these centrifuges. If the Western powers knew this, they would seek to destroy our work."

"And Israel would attempt to retaliate," Sabih added.

"Exactly," Jalili said. "We cannot divulge this information until our capacities are so great that they understand that to attack us would be suicide for them."

"Suicide?" Tarif joked. "Once we have the weaponry, they are already dead."

The five men laughed.

Jalili stood. "Let us celebrate as we stand on the eve of a great victory."

❖ ❖ ❖

Flight 755 cruised into Heathrow Airport with the lights of London beginning to sparkle beneath the darkening sky. Light sprinkles bounced against the windows of the 747 as it settled on the runway, turned, and rolled toward the gate.

Passengers jumped up from their seats and began grabbing bags from the overheads. Simone and Eric followed the line pressing to exit the airplane's side door. Many of the passengers hurried past, rushing toward the passport control area. Eric and Simone kept a leisurely pace.

The lines had already lengthened by the time they queued

up for passport control. Each person stood with documents in hand, some patiently, some not, inching their way toward the booth where an officer with a metal stamp sat ready to let them in or turn them aside.

They passed passport control and retrieved their bags off the conveyors. Pulling the luggage behind them, they quickly walked by the final control officer and out the exit door. A huge gathering of people stood outside the doors, waving at the passengers as they came out. Some people held up signs; others leaned against the barriers intently watching each person who walked by. Simone and Eric cut a straight path through the crowd.

"Follow me," she said. "There's an Irish pub straight ahead. O'Flanigans. We're meeting a friend."

"Ah, a great way to end the day."

Simone headed toward the back of the pub. In a rear booth, a man with a shaved head sat quietly chewing on an unlit cigar. An old sweatshirt and jeans made him look like an average lower-class British citizen. His forlorn eyes intensely studied Eric, but he remained motionless.

"*Boker tov*," Simone said and sat down.

"You brought a friend," Benny said.

"I decided Eric would be of value on the next phase of the trip. He's going with me."

Benny drew back. "Dragon man knows about this?"

"He will."

Benny eyed Eric critically. "He's a goyim?"

"It's unimportant whether he's Jewish or not. Stone's been in the intelligence business all of his life. He knows the ropes."

Benny shifted the cigar to the other side of his mouth. "You don't say."

"Yeah." Simone glared at him. "You got a problem?"

"I ain't the one you gotta please. But the fire-breathing man might get a little testy."

"He knows who Stone is."

"Well—there's a little problem here. The next stop on your itinerary is Cairo. I only got one ticket." He shoved the envelope across the table. "You gonna pack him in a bag? A Stone might prove to be a little heavy."

Simone ignored Benny's little joke. "We'll get him a ticket. How much time do we have, Benny?"

"Your flight leaves tomorrow morning. I suggest you get that ticket and buzz out of here. I leave for Israel tomorrow. I won't see you again."

"Nice seeing you again." Eric extended his hand.

Benny looked at it for a moment, shifted the cigar in his mouth, and finally shook it. "Yeah. Good luck." He slid out of the booth and walked away.

"Your friend Benny wasn't expecting to see me," Eric said.

"He wasn't. That's his problem, not ours. After we've purchased your ticket, I need to call Dar Dagan before Benny talks to him. I don't want Benny interpreting your presence before I explain matters." She started moving out of the booth. "Let's get that ticket."

After standing in line for twenty minutes, they purchased the ticket. The evening was lengthening and Simone knew she must call Tel Aviv. Seldom did she use Dagan's private cell phone number. Dagan wouldn't consider her situation a crisis, but Benny could turn it into one with a few innuendos. She punched in the numbers.

"*Shalom*," Simone began.

"Koole?" Dagan asked.

"Yes."

"What's gone wrong?"

"Nothing. However, there is one change you should be aware of. I am now traveling with a companion."

"Companion!" Dagan's voice raised. "What are you talking about?"

"Eric Stone from the Conundrum is accompanying me."

"Stone! Why is he there?"

"I have determined that I will probably face more complications than expected. I need his help."

"You've got a broken leg or something? You didn't get approval for this action."

"The Conundrum has exceptional connections across the Middle East. I determined—"

"*You* determined! Listen, you're pushing your luck again in no small way."

"You always told me to rely on my insight. I am. Stone's been doing this work for decades. I need his assistance. I've already purchased his ticket to Cairo. We leave in the morning."

A long silence oozed through the cell phone. Finally, Dagan said, "You better not have any complications."

Simone relaxed. "I don't plan on any. I'm expecting Stone to carry his weight."

"Then you have full responsibility for this decision. Got me?"

"I understand." Simone hung up.

Even though his involvement hadn't been in the plans, Eric was right. His presence might end up being crucial. Whether the dragon man liked it or not, it was a done deal.

Simone dropped the cell phone into her pocket. "Let's go to the hotel, Eric. It's been a long day."

40

Egypt Air flight 70 roared across Europe with a steady hum. Flight attendants walked the aisle, offering drinks and snacks while Simone and Eric dozed. She awoke first and glanced at her wristwatch. Making as little noise as possible, she pulled her shoulder bag from under the seat in front of her and began searching through the contents.

Eric opened one eye. "What are you doing, mystery woman?"

Simone smiled. "Time for me to turn into a Muslim. Simone Koole's not exactly the most welcome visitor in Egypt these days." She pulled a long black drape from the bag. "Wrapping myself in this little number starts the show." She shook the large covering and stuck her head through a hole in the middle. "These robes turn me into nothing but a fleeting shadow floating down the street." She took out a thickly woven cap and pulled it over her head and down her neck, causing her hair to disappear. She rubbed her lips with a tissue. "I have to look as plain as a white wall. No improvements on the face allowed."

She took another item out of the bag. "Once I get my

hijab across my cheeks, you won't even know it's me." She hooked the veil in place. "Hebrew and Arabic are so closely related that I have no trouble speaking without an accent. The Egyptian officers will believe I'm the genuine article."

Eric stretched. "I suppose we won't cross passport control together."

"You'll use one of your fake passports, and I am Arub El-Nin. I keep an Egyptian passport with me when I travel. Birthplace lists Cairo. Just a local girl returning home."

"Arub? Sounds like the name will work."

"When we get to the other side, stay behind me. I'll go outside and hail a taxi. You jump in just before it takes off."

"I understand."

"You've been to Cairo before?" Simone asked.

"Sure. Went to the pyramids once, but much of our work has been further east. Iraq, Iran, Afghanistan, Jordan, over there. Still, we get around. Conundrum has worked Egypt."

Simone grinned. "You've never seen the City of the Dead?"

"Afraid not."

"While we're waiting for our next instructions, I'll show you a sight you'll long remember. Come on. Let's get through customs."

⸎⸎⸎

Smells of spices and unusual foods filled the air. Men walked past wearing red fez caps. Eric stayed fifteen feet behind Simone while they wound through the crowded terminal. The Cairo airport was radically different from Heathrow Airport. Simone blended into the crowd of women in black robes exactly like hers. He had to pay attention as she moved quickly and merged into a collage of dark colors. Turning a corner, he recognized the exit ahead. Just beyond the door, cars maneuvered to break out of the eternal traffic jam. One car had five mattresses stacked and tied on top; another had no fenders. Beggars hovered around the walls with their hands out. Dirty children chased each other down the sidewalk.

"Cairo never changes," Eric mumbled.

Edging through the teeming multitude, Eric watched Simone grab a taxi. She opened the back door and turned to look for him. He rushed toward a dilapidated Ford that had to be thirty years old. Dented fenders and worn green paint added another ten years to the appearance. Eric hopped in and landed on a seat with worn cushions and holes in the upholstery. The driver steered the rolling disaster through the maze of traffic while Simone chattered in his ear. The cab driver kept nodding while flipping ashes from his cigarette out the window. Finally, she scooted back in the seat.

"We're on our way to the Cairo Necropolis," Simone said. "I thought you'd find the City of the Dead to be an unusual and interesting sight. You've seen so much of the world, but I bet this little excursion will be an adventure."

"Cairo's Necropolis . . . sounds like a trip through Halloween Land."

"You'll see."

The taxi rumbled down the broad highway until it took an abrupt turn down an access road. The broken asphalt and pitted street jarred the Ford back and forth violently, but the driver didn't slow. As they roared down a neighborhood street, the man kept blaring the horn. Anyone even hinting they might get close to the vehicle got a blast. He seldom slowed.

"Our driver would make a good kamikaze pilot," Eric declared.

"If we live through this ride," Simone said, "we'll come to more than a four-mile stretch that is nothing but solid mausoleums and burial sites. The houses and bungalows were originally constructed for the dead, but time has made some fascinating changes. Poor people now live in some of these structures. Urban renewal forced some to migrate to the cemetery. Living with your dead relatives doesn't sound inviting, but then again, where else were these people going to live?"

"This place must be huge. How long has it been here?"

"In 642 CE, the Arabs took control of Egypt and started the burial grounds. It's been here ever since."

The taxi pulled up to a large gateway and stopped. The driver pointed straight ahead and held his hand out.

"Now, we get to haggle." Simone immediately launched into a loud exchange with the driver.

Eric watched in amazement as Simone sounded like World War III was about to start. Finally, she paid the driver and slipped in a tip. An armistice was instantly declared, and the driver broke into a wide smile. They got out of the taxi.

"He looked happy," Eric said.

"In Cairo, a tip does the trick." She led him through the gate. "The Necropolis can be a rough place when they realize you're a tourist. Keep an eye on your back."

"Now you tell me?" Eric ambled down the narrow street.

"Some of these buildings have bodies stacked on top of bodies extending back for centuries. On special days of commemoration, families come to these buildings and hold picnics with the deceased tucked away beside them."

Ancient edifices lined the winding roadway. Many were crumbling but still being used for burials. At different turns in the street, they caught sight of people watching them from behind the cement doorways. One glance at the gawkers and the spying eyes disappeared behind the ancient walls.

"I think we're the main attraction today," Eric said. "The locals seem to be watching us. Are you concerned?"

Simone glanced around. "I'm afraid you're right, Eric. It looks like we might be raising suspicions."

"Yeah." Eric turned down a narrow alley. "And I don't have any idea where we are."

Two men stepped out of the shadows at the end of the alley and stared at them.

"Let's cut through this next building and take a different route." Simone stepped into the entryway and rushed toward the gaping hole in the wall.

Even though he didn't hesitate, Eric surveyed the drab large room as he hurried through. The ceramic tile floor looked like the pieces had been moved many times and then shoved back together. The whitewashed walls had tarnished streaks with paint peeling off in strips. Next to the far wall, a cement crypt with a long, thick lid appeared old and ominous.

"Jump through the opening," Simone said with more than her usual forcefulness.

Eric leaped onto the ledge and jumped through. He could hear footsteps racing down the street. "Let's go."

They twisted and turned down a rambling alleyway. Eric had no idea where they were or where they were going, but he kept running. The path turned to the right and opened into a much broader street. At the opposite end, two additional men stood in crouched position.

Simone stopped. "We've picked up two more bird dogs."

Eric straightened. "I want you to step back into the next building and do that exit routine again. Don't stop until you can't see these jerks."

"But—"

"Now!" Eric demanded. "Run."

Simone darted into the building, but Eric kept walking toward the hatchet men. "You boys want to tangle, come on," he said. "You think you scare me?"

The two men looked at each other with an unsteady glance. It appeared they hadn't expected him to come at them and weren't sure what to do next.

The man on the left took a step backward, but the other man said something harsh and stopped. They both crouched as if to imply that they might attack any moment. Eric kept walking straight toward them without slowing. The man on the left took off running, but his companion pulled a knife.

Starting to circle to his right, the attacker maneuvered his knife back and forth with slow swings. The blade looked like it might be six inches long and glistened in the sun. This guy meant business.

Eric didn't slow his steady pace and walked straight toward the attacker. The man kept blinking but didn't back off. Eric crouched and stopped less than ten feet from the swinging knife.

The man started jabbing in straightforward thrusts. Eric studied his movements. There wasn't style, a method; he simply used the knife to threaten. No doubt he'd stab, but he didn't have military skill. Eric crept forward, waiting for the right moment. The guy jabbed a little farther, and Eric realized he was off balance. Grabbing the man's wrist, Eric jerked him forward with a hard yank. The attacker sprawled on the street with his arm straight in front of him. Eric stomped on his hand. The man screamed, and the knife tumbled away. Before he could move, Eric dropped his knee into the middle of his back and grabbed his hair. After three hard yanks, Eric smashed his face into the pavement. The attacker didn't move.

Eric looked up and down the street, but the companion had disappeared. Simone had also vanished. Looking around carefully, he saw and heard nothing. Eric was alone in the midst of a vast mortuary filled with centuries-old corpses. He had no idea where he was, where he should turn, which way was out. Most important, what had become of Simone?

For the next two hours, he wandered up and down the strange, twisting streets that seemed to go nowhere. Each turn led to another obscure street in the bewildering maze. If he shouted, no telling who might turn up, or he could even jeopardize Simone. No matter which way he went, the buildings took on a vague, meaningless sameness. Eric was hopelessly lost.

Could the other two men have run Simone down? Eric knew not to panic, but he felt a sense of alarm. The clicking of his own leather shoes against the ancient pavement was all he heard. Another hour dragged by.

Even if he found his way out of this vast holding tank of coffins, where would he go? Simone hadn't told him where to meet her later if they got separated. Eric cursed himself for such a stupid error.

Eric moved on until he found a low wall where he could sit. He wiped the sweat from his neck with his handkerchief.

"There you are!"

Eric whirled around and saw Simone walking up behind him. "Simone!"

"I thought I'd never find you." She sat down next to him.

"How did you find me?"

"A little luck and that annoying click of your shoes did the trick." Simone hugged him. "I worried that the street warriors might have bested you."

"What about those two guys that followed you?"

Simone shrugged. "They caught up with me by swinging around behind a couple of buildings. I suspect they thought a woman would make an easy target."

"And?"

"They're probably still lying on the street. If I'm good at anything, it's fighting with amateurs. I'm sure they both have broken bones."

"Okay. What do we do now?"

"I got a phone call from Benny Gantz. He didn't even mention Dar Dagan, which means he'd talked to him and discovered that I beat him to the punch. Benny gave me the directions for the next leg of our trip."

Eric gestured for her to continue. "And?"

"We need to get out of here and get a taxi. We're going to the Suez Canal."

"You're kidding."

"There's a tramp freighter coming across this evening. The ship's our ticket south."

41

The fierce heat of the day faded as the sun drifted over the Nile River. Even with night approaching, large freighters continued cruising the Suez Canal's hundred-mile stretch connecting the Mediterranean Sea with the Gulf of Suez.

Standing on Port Said's dock, Eric observed the wear of time. The eleven to sixteen hours it took to travel from one end to the other was nothing compared to how long it would have taken to sail around Africa.

Simone had been gone forty-five minutes making sure they got on the right freighter. She should be back by now. Eric tapped a text to George that he was standing at the Suez Canal waiting for a ship. A response came back quickly.

Got it. Good. Not sure where you're going. Glad you're secure.

Heard from Jack? Eric responded.

Just got a report. He's now in Syria. Looks like Syria is edging toward a full-scale civil war. Their third largest city Homs has entered a new phase. Armed civilians are fighting the security forces. Appears bad.

Tell Jack to stay alert, Eric texted. *May need him soon.*

I will.

Eric put his cell phone back in his pocket. George would keep the Conundrum machine running at home. Sarah would undoubtedly harass him on a daily basis, but nothing new there.

"Hey!" Simone walked hurriedly down the dock.

"What's the deal?" Eric asked.

"As soon as this freighter goes by, the next ship will tie up to let some of its crew off while taking on new hands. We'll board then. Every detail has been cleared. Follow me and I'll take you down to our quarters."

"Expect any problems?"

Simone raised an eyebrow. "I didn't this morning and look what that little adventure got us. I'm sorry, Eric. I wanted to show you a fascinating place, but things went terribly wrong."

"Let's hope not to repeat that."

Simone squeezed his hand. "I'm glad you're with me. I've always been a totally independent operator, but you've made a few changes in my routine. Feels good to have you beside me."

"We're both traveling on a new path." Eric kissed her.

"Okay. We're going to board momentarily. Do you realize what today is?"

Eric thought for a moment. "Friday?"

"When the sun goes down, it's the Sabbath."

"And?"

"The Sabbath is a special night for Jews. We light candles. Break the bread. Drink the wine. Pray. When we get to our cabins, I will start the observance. I hope you will join me."

"Of course. But I have no idea what to do."

"I'll show you. Let's line up to board the ship."

They walked across the dock while workers came and went in every direction. Many of the men wore long robes; others dressed in the rough garb of laborers. A ship with the paint peeling off churned into the loading zone flying a Turkish flag with the name SS *Aswan* painted on the bow. The narrow channel didn't allow two ships to pass at the same time so traffic was always delayed while the one-way zone managed the flow of traffic. The SS *Aswan* threw the engines in reverse and brought the ship to a halt. A crew member cranked out a rough gangplank that bumped and scraped the dock when it landed. Within minutes, the loading process had begun. A sailor carrying a clipboard trotted down the ramp and posted himself at the base. "Loading time!" the man shouted.

"Let's hurry!" Simone pulled Eric's hand. "Get on as quickly as we can."

By the time they lined up, four men already stood in front of them, but the line moved quickly.

The sailor ran down his list. "You're Arub El-Nin?"

Simone nodded her head.

"Got a passport?"

She held it up.

The seaman didn't even look at it. "Next."

Eric held his passport by his face.

Again, the officer only glanced at the passport to catch the name. "Next."

Once on board, Simone steered them down three flights of stairs. "Since Benny set this cruise up, we're certainly not first class. Good ol' Benny stuffed us down here based on the theory that obscurity provides the greatest security."

"And also a little reward for outflanking him with Dar Dagan."

Simone laughed. "We play these little games to keep our sanity. Like Sarah and George. The dragon man knows about those jokes and tries to stay aloof, but he understands." She looked at her watch. "The sun's almost completely gone. I got our room numbers when I checked in. Throw your gear in the room marked 332. I'll be across the hall in 331."

When Eric pushed the steel door open, it banged against the railing of a narrow metal bed attached to the ship's wall. The room allowed almost no space to turn around. A small two-drawer chest had been pushed against the wall. The squeeze minimized everything. At most, he could lie on the thin mattress and pray that the ship didn't plow into a rough sea. Eric hung his shoulder bag on a hanger welded to the wall and slipped his jacket off. After shutting the door behind him, he crossed over and knocked on 331.

"Come in," Simone said. "I'm almost ready."

Two candles stood on top of her two-drawer chest. Simone had covered her head with a small lace scarf. On the bed, a round bun had been placed on top of a napkin and another scarf covered it. At the side, a pocketknife lay with the blade open. For the first time in days, she looked at him without the usual tenderness in her eyes.

"We are ready to begin." Simone picked up a matchbox. "Unfortunately, I don't have any other way to make a flame, but this will do." She struck the match and began lighting the first candle. Her voice intoned a simple Jewish melody. "Blessed are you, Lord our God, King of the universe, who has sanctified us with his commandments, and commanded us to kindle the light of the holy Shabbat." As she began singing in Hebrew, Simone bent over the candles and rotated her hands as if drawing the smoke toward her face. Her voice seemed to shift and come from another place.

Eric watched, saying nothing.

Simone kept humming and looked almost like she had drifted into another world. "Observe and remember; the Lord is One and his Name is One, for renown, for glory, and for praise." Her voice stayed low almost in a guttural groan. Finally, it faded away.

"You may cut the bread," she said to Eric.

Taking the small knife, Eric cut the bun in two pieces. Simone pulled a small saltshaker out of her pocket and salted each piece. She began eating and nodded for Eric to do the same. After a few minutes, the bread was gone.

Her eyebrows abruptly drew together and she looked away. Eric watched, unsure of why her countenance had changed. Without saying a word, she blew out the candles and set them to one side. She carefully scraped the bread crumbs into her hand and pulled the scarf from her head.

"I'll see you later, Eric."

"What?"

She closed the cabin door behind her and was gone.

42

The sway of the freighter awakened Eric. Sleeping beneath the vessel's waterline, he had no way to see out, but he was sure they had sailed into the Sea of Suez and were on their way into the Red Sea that divided Egypt and Saudi Arabia. The walls weren't soundproof, but he had heard no noise in the hallway.

Simone must be up by now. Eric couldn't guess what must be wrong. There'd been no argument, no fight. She had disappeared without a word.

He sat up in the narrow bed and flipped the lights on. The grayness of the walls and the floor gave the room a foreboding quality. No pictures. No decorations. Plain old plainness.

Something was different with Simone, and it bothered him that he had no idea what had changed. Her unexplained silence kept shouting in his face.

Eric rolled out of bed and quickly dressed. Whether she liked it or not, he had to know what was going on. If he needed to turn the ship inside out and upside down to locate her, he would. Eric crossed the hall and knocked on her door. The salty smell of the sea filled his nose, but nothing more touched his senses except the feeling of emptiness. He pounded harder. No response.

Eric hurried down the hall and up the stairs. He passed seamen, but they only nodded at most. He didn't want any conversations where language became an issue. On the next floor up, he grabbed an elevator to take him up to the food deck level.

Lining up with other men waiting to pass the serving tables, he kept scrutinizing the large dining area. At the far end of the room, Simone sat eating alone with the worn captain's hat pulled over her forehead. Men ate at the other end of the table, but no one was close to her. At the least, he could sit across from her and talk.

The grub line moved slowly. One server scooped up scrambled eggs and dumped them onto a plate. The next one dropped two sausages next to the eggs. The last attendant slopped a serving spoon of soupy beans and a whole stewed tomato in the remaining space. Looked like an English breakfast on a bad day.

When he turned around, Simone had disappeared. Undoubtedly, she had seen him coming through the line. He put the tray on the table and scooted into his chair. Her abrupt departure only deepened the mystery. Maybe Simone had some new information that disturbed her. Could she have received a communiqué from Tel Aviv?

He had to find Simone and press her for an answer.

After scraping his plate clean, he shoved the utensils through the return window into the kitchen area. He dropped a paper napkin into the large trash bin and started down the hall. Simone might be avoiding him, but she couldn't hide in most of the rooms because the doors were locked. The deck had a few chairs, but that was such an obvious area he could spot her quickly. Still, it was worth a look.

He got into the elevator and descended to the main deck. The hot desert sun had already begun to bear down, and no breeze drifted across the hull. Just as he suspected, Simone wasn't there. Walking quickly, he made a complete circle of the platform. Nothing.

He returned to the elevator, descended to the bottom of the ship, and started his search back up the decks to the top level. Like a hike through the mountains on an obscure trail, climbing from one level to the next proved arduous. Only after he reached the top of the ship did he pause. Of course, he couldn't enter the women's shower area at the end of the top flight for a peek. He could sit outside and wait for her to come out, but that would probably prove pointless. Where could she have . . .

Eric abruptly realized why a shower would be at the top of the ship. There must be an exercise room nearby where the sailors worked out when they were off duty. Simone maintained a rigorous routine to keep her topflight condition. He started down the hall in the opposite direction. Reaching the end of the hall, he heard the sound of rapid footfalls. Opening the door, he saw only one person working out.

Running at a fast clip on a treadmill, Simone had a towel around her neck and a determined look on her face. The roar of the machine drowned out any other sound. She must have been running for some time to have developed such a sweat. Eric slipped behind her and waited for her to stop. After five minutes, she pushed the off button, and the machine slowed to a halt. Simone wiped her face and stepped off.

"Good morning," Eric said.

Simone jumped. "What!"

"Been watching you run away from me. On the machine. Down the halls. In the dining room. Everywhere. Running."

Simone took a step backward. "I don't want to talk."

"I do."

"Please."

"No."

She took a deep breath. "Eric, this is impossible."

"What is 'this'?"

"Okay." Simone's entire body sagged. "Let's sit down over there." She gestured toward several chairs against the wall.

Eric swung one of the chairs around facing the other and sat down. Simone sat opposite him. For a long time, they looked at each other without speaking.

"Last night," Simone started and then stopped. After a moment, she began again. "When I lit the candles and said the prayers, I was repeating a ritual that my people have done for thousands of years. I know it didn't seem like much to you, but it touched a nerve, my core. I was reminded who I am and who you are."

"Who I am? What does that have to do with anything?"

"It has to do with *everything*. You are a goyim, a Gentile. You are the rest of the world outside of Israel. Our people have always cared for the well-being of others, about the stranger at the door. But Jews stick together. We are a race unto ourselves." She paused for a long moment. "We should only marry other Jews."

Eric didn't know what to say.

"The candlelight reminded me that my first priority is the well-being of my people. I know that is true for you, but it is even more important for me. I cannot let a relationship with a Gentile obscure my focus. You and I can be colleagues, but never more. I need to put some distance between us. For the rest of this trip, we are intelligence agents working together, but nothing more."

"But Simone—"

Simone squeezed her eyes shut. "My assignment takes precedence over everything. I'm sorry." She slung the towel around her neck and walked determinedly out of the gym.

Eric stared at the door closing behind her.

43

Another day dragged by while the freighter maneuvered down the Strait of Suez. Eric watched the barrenness of the Sinai Peninsula slide by. To the west not too far away stood Jabal Katrina, the supposed location of Mt. Sinai where Moses received the Ten Commandments. At the end of the peninsula the Sharm-el-Sheik settlement housed a United Nations garrison that had once guarded the waterways.

The bleak scenery matched his feelings. Simone had left him marooned on an emotionally empty island. Granted, their relationship had developed too fast. Still, he would have been glad to talk about any reservations she had. Of course, their assignment took precedence, but he could see no reason for retreat from their relationship. Simone didn't see things that way. No matter which way he walked, she went in the opposite direction.

Wind and hammering rainstorms had beaten on the barren, rolling mountains lining the desert and carved deep ravines for countless centuries. Deep cracks gave the terrain a foreboding raggedness. The Old Testament said Jews had first come this way in their flight from Egypt. The Hebrews had been a hearty lot to have meandered through the stark, dry valleys making their way to the Promised Land. Simone's family descended from such stock. The struggles of both the grandparents and the parents reflected a tenacity that had been passed down to her. Eric knew if she made up her mind to do something, nothing would hinder her course.

"Ah-lan!" A dark-skinned sailor wearing a captain's hat moseyed alongside him. The dirty T-shirt had Arabic script across the front. His blue jeans looked old and stained.

Eric nodded pleasantly.

"Kefy heh-lak?"

"I am fine," Eric said in English. "Sorry. I don't speak Arabic."

"Oh!" the man said. "You sound American."

Eric studied him carefully. This character wasn't just being friendly. He'd pulled alongside to check him out. "Really?"

The sailor said nothing but looked out over the sea. "Beautiful country."

Eric shrugged. "You have to like desert."

"Right are you. You like desert?"

"Sure." Eric kept looking straight ahead.

"Not many sail down to Yemen. Dangerous place for American."

"I don't read the newspapers," Eric said. "Wouldn't know."

The sailor's eyes narrowed and he walked away.

The guy wasn't just fishing for tuna, Eric thought. Whether she wanted to talk or not, Simone needed to know about the exchange.

He got on the elevator and rode up to the top level to the gym. Maybe she'd be there; maybe she wouldn't. It was the best place to begin a search. Opening the heavy metal door, he found her running on the treadmill.

Simone looked up and hit the off button.

"I was just approached by one of the crew. Guy dressed like a sailor but wearing a captain's hat somewhat like yours. T-shirt with Arabic script. Not the tidiest guy I've seen around the boat. He might have been just making conversation, but I don't think so."

Simone's eyes narrowed. She pulled a cell phone out of her workout suit and punched in numbers. When the other party answered, she began speaking Hebrew. For five minutes the conversation went back and forth with long pauses interspersed with chatter. He could tell the hard look on her face reflected concern. Finally, she clicked off.

"Benny ran the ship's register. He doesn't have a clue about the man's identity. It's possible the Egyptians placed security guards to float down the Red Sea checking people out. If the man gets off when we dock at Yanbu, Saudi Arabia, that's what he's probably all about. If he's still on board after that, we may have a problem that we'll have to attend to." Simone slung a towel around her neck and walked out.

44

During the day that followed their conversation in the gym, Eric didn't see Simone. Even with a large ship, they should have run into each other, but Simone was clever enough to have figured out an area that concealed her. By evening, he let the chase go. The situation was what it was. He had to live with it.

The following morning, the freighter churned toward Port Yanbu, an obscure docking point on the edge of Saudi Arabia. The holy city of Medina stood due east a couple of hundred miles, and Mecca lay over four hundred miles straight south. The ship's path led them toward the heart of Muslim holy land where the Saudis took their desert territory seriously. A good region for no slipups.

Eric stood on the deck of the ship and watched the vessel ease toward Yanbu. The pressing issue was what Mr. Big Nose would do when the ship tied up. Eric stood at the rail watching for him. Only one ramp would lead to the dock. If the man wearing a captain's hat came down, Eric would see him.

The freighter's loud blast alerted the port, and men began running toward the loading zone. Seawater splashed against the ship, sending up a sour smell, but Eric couldn't see garbage below. The crew worked in a systematic manner to secure the mooring. Men hurled huge, thick ropes to the dock, and workers quickly secured the vessel. Other laborers hauled wooden crates and large boxes across the pier. Finally, the sound of the ramp being cranked down rang out. The metal incline clanked against the thick wood of the long harbor as it fell into position.

Several crew members walked down with papers in hand and started checking the goods lined up on the wharf. Other dock workers began hauling containers up the ramp. Eric watched more intently. No sign of Mr. Big Nose.

For an hour, the mariners hauled cargo into the hold of the freighter. Finally, the ship's supervisors signaled that loading had been completed and raised the ramp. In record time, the process reversed itself and the craft began its journey back into the Red Sea. Yanbu had been a brief stop. Only one thing had been clarified: they had a problem.

❖-❖-❖

That evening, Simone turned up in the dining room. Much to Eric's surprise, she seemed to be looking for him. He kept walking through the serving line while she sat at her usual rear position near the back wall, not moving a muscle, staring at him. He returned a silent glance meant to communicate "sit tight."

As always, a server dropped a scoop of mashed potatoes onto Eric's metal tray. The next slipped in a hefty piece of meat. Finally, Eric picked up a mug of steamy coffee and headed for the back.

Simone said nothing when he sat down. Without any comment, he began eating. He could tell she kept staring at him.

"The T-shirt with Arabic script didn't show," Simone said.

"Right."

"Benny texted me. He's identified the individual. His name is Sadeq al-Amar. Works out of Egypt for Hamas. Benny thinks Sadeq may be on my tail. Could be wrong. If he's right, the man will attempt to assassinate me. Do you see him in this room?"

Eric turned and slowly studied the men sitting across the dining hall. "I don't see him in here."

"Does he look like this?" Simone held up her cell phone. A man's face appeared on the screen.

"That's the guy."

"I'm afraid we have a problem. Sadeq al-Amar has not been able to locate me all day, but tonight I'm sure he'll be back at it. In the time it's taken us to identify him, he's probably done so with me. We must assume I'm the assassin's target, and he won't wait long to strike."

Eric's jaw tightened.

"Here's the plan," Simone said. "Our buddy Sadeq hasn't seen us together for a couple of days, and he's not in here now. In a moment, I'm going to take my tray to the trash. I'll stand outside the door for three minutes. You follow me."

Eric took a deep breath. "That puts you in a vulnerable position."

"Not as much as you might think. I have an Israeli Desert Eagle .357 tucked in my belt. One blast and our boy is history."

"If, and I repeat *if*, you get him first. But if he strikes from behind—"

225

"That's your job, Eric. If he gets behind me, you've got to get him first."

"I don't like any of this."

"Listen to me carefully. If this assassin should kill me, you'll find a USB storage device in my quarters, taped on the top of the first drawer in the one small chest. You are to contact Benny Gantz, and he'll tell you what to do next. His number is in there too. Understand me? This project could end up in your hands."

Eric swallowed hard and gritted his teeth.

"Do exactly as I've told you. I'm going to leave now and walk down to the outside deck. Watch my back." Simone stood up and hurried away.

45

Eric got up quickly and carried his tray to the kitchen's disposal area. Three minutes had not passed, but he worried that he might not be positioned quickly enough. Walking out in front of this Hamas assassin amounted to throwing herself in front of a train to slow it down. But Eric knew he would have done the same thing.

Stepping into the dim hallway, Eric saw Simone standing at the far end, starting to descend the stairs. The stairway had been well lighted and allowed no dark corners.

Midway down, Simone came to the deck level and went outside. Night was falling, and it wouldn't be easy to see every corner of the ship. He'd have to move stealthily to stay in the shadows while watching her back. Unfortunately, the assassin could fire from an obscure angle and be gone before Eric came close. Simone could have set herself up for disaster.

The wind picked up and blew the door shut behind him. The ship rocked more than usual. A strong gale and the sway made him even more nervous. What had Simone been thinking? Sticking herself out there in plain sight amounted to waving a red flag at a bull.

Slowly, he crept toward a three-foot-high metal container that probably held life jackets. If nothing else, he could stand behind the long receptacle and still hide beneath the overhang. From that angle he could see her standing next to the ship's railing. The position wasn't ideal, but it would work.

Simone stood there looking out over the ocean. She appeared totally unconcerned that at any moment she could be dead.

Pain shot through Eric's neck, and suddenly he couldn't breathe. A rope tightened around his throat. He grabbed at the cord, but it only tightened. His knees buckled and his heart pumped overtime. The assassin had been standing in the shadows against the ship's hull. He must have obscured the man's view when he stepped behind the metal chest, and thus become the immediate target. The tightening noose said he would be on the deck dead in a couple of minutes.

With the heel of his shoe, Eric stomped on the man's foot. Bones cracked. The guy screamed and loosened his grip. Swinging his elbow as hard as he could, Eric caught him in the ribs. The noose dropped. With his free hand, Eric grabbed the man's belt, hoisted him up, and slung the assailant over his shoulder. Al-Amar hit the top of the metal container and bounced over to the deck, sprawling flat. Eric came overtop and leaped on him, cramming an elbow into the man's back. An excruciating agony abruptly surged through Eric's body. His head throbbed and a blinding pain disrupted his sight. The man had smashed him in the most vulnerable part of his body. For a moment, paralysis swallowed Eric. His arms dangled immobile at his side. The Palestinian grabbed his hair and yanked his head back; a noose went around Eric's neck again. Eric knew he didn't have the strength to fight the attacker off. No matter how he tried to gulp air, he couldn't breathe, and his head began to swim.

"Aaah!" Al-Amar screamed and let go.

Out of the corner of his eye, Eric recognized someone pulling the man backward. He could barely turn his head but realized the attacker had been pushed to the railing. In one heave, his body went sailing over the edge. A moment later, Eric heard the splash. Rolling to his side, he tried to get up, but his legs wouldn't respond.

Two hands slipped under his arms and pulled. "Try it again," Simone said. "You can make it."

He pushed himself up on his knees and shook his head, trying to clear his mind, but the ship seemed to sway wildly.

"I'm going to help you walk," Simone said. "Lean on me."

"I'll try." He staggered forward.

"We're going to get in the elevator. Hang on to me."

Once inside the lift, Eric still found it difficult to stand up.

"If anyone says anything, mumble that you had one too many," Simone said. "Men get drunk around here all the time. They won't ask you anything more."

The elevator descended to the cabin level. Simone pushed him through the opening door and guided him down the hall.

"I'm going to take you to your room." She reached in his pocket for the key. "I want you to lie down. Take it easy."

"Yeah."

Once past the door, she swung him onto the bed. Eric rubbed his eyes, trying to focus on the ceiling, which seemed to move in a slanting, shifting direction. "What happened?"

"Al-Amar was going down for the count when he put a

knee in your groin and a Zap in the back of your head. Your lights had almost gone out when he slipped that strangle cord back around your neck."

"You killed him."

"I hate to tell you this, but I figured he'd come after you first. I wasn't brave as much as I was confident in what this scumbag would do. Honestly, I didn't think you'd have much of a problem taking him. Turned out worse than I thought. I am sorry."

Eric heard her words but found it difficult to tie them together. "Me first?" he mumbled.

"I believed the guy would be more obvious and you'd lay him out. Thank God we were close to each other. Don't worry. He's gone and won't be coming back."

Eric sank into the pillow. The back of his head throbbed, his body ached, and he still felt dizzy.

"Thanks for saving me." He'd barely gotten the words out before he passed out.

46

Eric awoke to only a dim glow from a small lamp lighting the bunk room. For a few moments, he wasn't sure where he was. The dull grayness of the room didn't feel familiar, but then again, it seemed like he'd been there before. He raised his head slowly, but the back of his head throbbed. His eyes slowly focused, but the room still looked blurry.

"Where am I?"

"In your cabin," Simone said.

"Simone? You're here?"

"I am."

"I don't remember what happened." Eric thought for a moment. "We struggled . . . on the deck. I was attacked. Yes, I remember now. Got hit."

"Yes."

"Last night?"

"No," Simone said, "three nights ago."

"Three?"

"The attacker hit you on the head with a leather-lined Zap. Hit you hard. Because you're in excellent condition, you didn't pass out until we returned to your cabin. Eric, you had a concussion and a more serious injury than you realized."

"A concussion?"

Simone laid her hand on his forehead. "You were also running a fever. It's gone now. I think you're going to be okay, but you need to rest."

"Three nights ago?" Eric reached for her hand. "You've been here for the entire time."

"Of course."

He pushed himself up but could only see a faint outline of her against the light. "You've taken care of me?"

"Yes."

"Simone, you saved my life."

"You saved my life, Eric. We're even."

"No, we couldn't ever be . . ." The words wouldn't come out of his mouth. Eric drifted away.

⋯⋯⋯

When Eric awoke again, the room looked as it had earlier. The small lamp cast the same long shadows. Had he been asleep an hour, a day? The only thing that was evident was that the pain in the back of his head had diminished into a minor ache. He no longer felt dizzy or his thoughts disjointed. A second glance revealed Simone's absence. Eric swung his legs out of bed and sat up. His feet connected, but standing up took a bit more time. He needed a shower.

Hobbling around the small room revealed that a few aches remained from the struggle on the deck. After grabbing a towel and putting on a terry-cloth robe, he shuffled down the hall to the men's shower. The smell of soap and shampoo mingled with steaming water invigorated his body. With the hot spray running down his face, for the first time he fully realized how close he had come to being killed. While he didn't know exactly what had followed, Simone had sustained him through the close call.

If only she'd open her eyes to how much he owed her. Eric knew he'd have to play by her rules. He'd stay on his side of the line and not press her, but that didn't change how he felt.

He dried his hair cautiously to avoid the injury and put the robe back on. Time to get back in the game. Slinging the towel around his neck, he left the shower room and stepped out into the hall. Thirty feet away, Simone stood watching him.

"You look much better," she said. "I think you'll live."

"I'm afraid to ask, but how long did I sleep this time?"

"An entire day has passed. It's evening again. We are now in the Gulf of Aden and sailing past Yemen."

"Yemen!"

Simone shook her head. "You missed the fun when they discovered al-Amar had disappeared. They even looked in your room while you were sleeping. It appears the ship's crew didn't know his purpose and concluded he jumped ship along the way. It's over now."

She immediately turned and walked away.

47

The sun had begun to set when Eric strolled out on the freighter's deck. A few men still worked mopping the floor and moving a few chairs around. Heat from the desert winds had not subsided, and the dry warmth surrounded him like a blanket. Although the wind remained hot, it felt good. He strolled over to the railing, looked over the edge, and watched the ocean churn beneath the bow. Waves fanned out over the rolling tide and disappeared beyond the ship. The peacefulness of the sea felt reassuring. Pain had slipped away and he felt rested.

The door opened behind him. Simone walked determinedly across the ship toward him. Her old sailor's cap and the worn sweatshirt obscured her natural beauty. Without makeup, her naturally dark skin radiated its own magnetism.

"Hello, sunshine," Eric said and smiled.

Simone's eyes hardened. "We must talk. I hope you're feeling up for this."

Eric dropped any attempt to be familiar. "I think the concussion is behind me. I'm ready for action."

"You'll need all the strength you can muster for what's

ahead of us." Simone's voice remained flat and factual. "The real fun will begin shortly."

"Simone," Eric said with affection returning to his voice, "before you say anything more, I want to thank you for looking after me. I don't know how I'd have managed without you."

"I'd do the same for any colleague." Simone's response sounded like a doctor explaining a prescription. Direct, to the point, no emotion.

Eric ignored her businesslike tone. "When this is all over, I'd like to talk about us."

"There is no 'us,' Eric. Do you speak French?"

Eric shook his head.

"The French have a perfect word for where I am. The expression is called *désamour*. The exact meaning is nearly untranslatable in English, but the word means something like falling out of love or disenchantment. I find *désamour* says it all. Leave it at that."

Eric studied her face. Simone seemed to be intent upon throttling his affection with an iron fist. There was nothing he could say. Whatever romantic hopes he'd had were dying.

Simone turned and looked out over the water. "When we stopped at the last port, a chest was hauled on board loaded with the cargo. Inside, we'll find scuba equipment and wet suits. We will jump overboard when the ship approaches the next port, which will be in Iran."

"Swim to shore?"

Simone nodded. "I'll tell you the rest when we get closer. How quickly we move will depend on the speed of this ship, which is, of course, unpredictable, I'll let you know." She walked away.

Eric felt foolish. He had reached out to her once again, and she had turned him off like a radio. He had to conclude that their time together at Evergreen Lake had only been an apparition, a misreading, a mistake. He should have maintained the stance he'd held through the years, keeping an emotional distance from any woman. Maybe Simone was only playing him for a fool. Could be one of her strategies. Maybe she never cared about him in the first place.

He needed to just stuff his feelings and keep his eyes focused on the business at hand.

48

Eric sat in the dining hall eating lunch. Two days had passed since his last conversation with Simone. He had quit trying to run her down and spent most of his time on deck watching the bleak landscape drift by. The ship sailed on through the Arabian Sea, then turned the corner and cruised up the Gulf of Oman, only kilometers from Iran. The barren sameness of the eroded desert beaches eventually became boring, and he began reflecting on the strangeness of this trek.

Without warning, the American government had turned their guns on the Conundrum, hurling the organization into a chase Eric didn't understand. Dan had been killed in London, and his vacancy would not be filled. Eric's staff had been dispatched across several continents and shot at like moving targets in a carnival gallery. Out of this chaos had come a romance he had never planned on, yet it ended before it began. With little explanation, Simone had told him he was about to jump into the Strait of Hormuz and swim into one of the most hostile countries in the world. If they were caught in Iran, they'd both be shot on sight.

Seagulls circled above the ship. Land wasn't far away. The freighter had to be close to some port, but since Simone had said nothing more, he could only guess.

"Don't turn around," a woman's voice said behind him. Simone had crept up on him. Trying to prove a point?

"We are very close to the island of Qeshm," she said. "We will be sailing past the eastern tip of the land strip only two kilometers from the mainland. The ship is going to dock in Bandar Abbas. We will slip away when the freighter comes close to Qeshm."

"Someone is watching us?"

"Possibly."

Eric nodded. "Okay."

"In an hour and a half, I will meet you in my quarters. We will depart shortly."

After several moments of silence, Eric looked around, and she was gone. Several seamen stood on the deck above him looking out into the sea. Probably meant nothing. Could mean everything. Simone made few mistakes. She'd probably seen them up there.

He pulled his cell phone out of his pocket and began typing a message to George. Some of their agents were working in Iraq. At the least, he could try to tell George the latest development.

On the Strait of Hormuz. Will drop off on Qeshm Island shortly on the northeast tip of the island. Heads up.

Eric sent the message. After several minutes, he concluded nothing was coming back.

Off in the distance, he saw the outline of mountains beginning to appear above the horizon. Iran's terrain appeared to be more pleasant than Saudi Arabia's desert had been. Not far ahead, he saw an island. Had to be Qeshm.

Time to go downstairs and see what Simone had cooked up.

The elevator dropped quickly. Since it was midafternoon, the crew was working. No one stood around in the hall. He quickly walked to her door and knocked.

"*Keyf heh-lak?*" Simone asked in Arabic.

Eric recognized the phrase. "It's me."

"Come in," Simone said in English.

Her room was filled with diving equipment. Two wet suits were laid out on the bed. Oxygen tanks stood by the wall. Fins and flippers lay on the floor.

"I hauled this assortment up from the cargo room during the last couple of days. In forty-five minutes we'll be near the beach. We're going up three flights of stairs and out a side door that opens at ocean level. It's going to take some coordination, but I've got the equipment ready. You'll carry some of the equipment up in that black trunk, then come back down for the oxygen tanks. Once we open the ship's door, we're out of here. Got it?"

Eric watched her eyes. Not hard, but intensely determined. All business. No slack.

"Understood," he said.

"I want you to go over to your room and get rid of everything. I mean *everything*. It all goes."

Eric nodded. "What do we do about clothes when we swim to Qeshm?"

"We will then swim on to the shore near Bandar Abbas, the seaport in Iran. It's only a couple of kilometers from Qeshm. Supplies will be waiting."

"Our target is Bandar?"

"Yes. The city is the main base of the Iranian navy. No small operation. Perfect for our intentions."

"And the USB port device that brought us here?"

Simone reached inside her shirt and pulled out a chain with a pouch on the end. "If I am shot or killed, you are to retrieve this waterproof bag. Inside you'll find the flash drive with instructions. The most important task in your life is to complete this mission. Leave me where I fall." She dropped the container back into her shirt.

Eric wasn't sure he could do that, but he didn't protest. "So this has been our goal all along?"

Simone nodded. "Because of their navy bases in the Bandar Abbas port, the computer connections are perfect for our objective. We will plug it in and save the lives of millions of people."

49

The air tank bore down on Eric's shoulders. The weight of the metal container would help him stay well under the surface once they were in the Strait of Hormuz. At the moment, it only felt like a huge lead sinker.

"I'll unlock the exit door," Simone said. "After you're out, I'll swing it closed when I jump. If we do this right, nobody will notice we're gone until long after the ship docks. Maybe a day or two from now, they'll miss us."

"Got ya."

Simone flipped the safety lock and rotated the wheel that released the exit. With a final tug, the door cracked open. "We're not far from Qeshm Island."

"Won't be a long swim." Eric pointed across the waves lapping at the boat's side. "I'm ready."

He slipped over the edge and dropped into the sea. Simone slammed the door shut as she jumped.

She pointed toward the island and disappeared beneath the waves. The air tank immediately pulled him down to a twenty-foot level. The ocean appeared amazingly transparent with multicolored tropical fish darting through the coral reef jutting up from the bottom far below. After swimming a hundred feet, Eric realized that a shelf was starting to rise beneath them. Swimming over the marine terrain, he noticed much deeper holes in the coral reef. The dark shapes held a fascination that could have kept him gliding along the ocean bottom for days, but he kept swimming.

Eventually, the coral gave way to a sandy bottom. Eric watched Simone effortlessly swim forward even after the water was only three feet deep. Finally, she poked her head through the surf and pulled the diving mask up on her forehead.

"Turn off the oxygen," she whispered to Eric. "We might need the supply later. We'll sit here for a while and make sure no one is walking around the beach."

Eric watched the freighter steaming into the harbor. The exit door had stayed shut. So far, so good.

After thirty minutes, Simone stood up and walked ashore with her fins in hand. "We're going to walk the beach until we get to the other side of the island. Shouldn't be far away."

"It's still afternoon. We'll be swimming in sunlight on to the mainland?"

Simone shook her head. "We'll wait until sunset. I know where we're headed even in the dark." She picked up the pace.

⋯⋯⋯

The sun had begun to set, spreading shadows along the beach. No one had appeared and Simone said little, answering his questions with clipped sentences. The sparse conversation had dwindled into silence.

Eric watched the waves wash up on the beach. The long

walk had given him a lot of time to think. Most of his day-to-day work happened almost mechanically. He knew where to send his spies, what information he could trust, what he could write off as propaganda. He practiced martial arts until they were second nature. But working with Simone touched something deeper, something not on autopilot. Listening to Simone explain her faith had awakened his awareness of how God had guided his life through the years. More than he had realized in the past, he knew he had escaped death many times only because of God's intervention. They were about to swim into the mouth of the whale again. If ever he needed the eye of the Almighty on him, it was now.

Closing his eyes, Eric prayed silently. *God, thank you for pulling me out of the fire more times than I can count. I know I haven't been as faithful as I should have been over the years. Only your love could overlook my arrogance. Please forgive me.* He took a deep breath. *I'd sure appreciate it if you'd protect me one more time. Please help us to complete this assignment because it might make the world a better place. I'd certainly thank you and will try to do a better job of paying attention to what you ask. Amen.*

"I think it's dark enough," Simone said. "Our rendezvous point is about two kilometers across the open sea. Since the water is calm, we won't have any problem getting there. My compass wristwatch gives all the direction we need. I don't think we'll require oxygen, but I'll let you know if we need to turn it on. Stay close." She stood up and walked straight into the ocean, pausing only to put her fins on.

Eric skimmed behind her. Maintaining an easy pace, they bobbed along on the surface. Darkness settled over the strait, but Simone kept swimming toward some destination only she could identify. Eventually, their feet touched bottom and they walked ashore. Explaining nothing but watching her compass, she walked up the beach toward a small hut. Eric kept making sure no one observed them. Simone resolutely marched them into the shack and closed the door made of old boards nailed together haphazardly. She bent down and pulled up a section of the wooden floor made to function like a door.

"Please bring up that small trunk," Simone said. "It's got our clothing inside."

Eric worked the three-by-four container loose and set it on the floor. Opening the lid, he found a large black bundle and a burka sitting on top. Below he recognized a Revolutionary Guard uniform.

"You're about to become a soldier, and I'm a poor widow," Simone said. "Let's get this stuff on quickly. We'll put our wet suits and gear in the trunk for our return." She threw the large black drape over her head and shed the wet suit.

Underneath the uniform, Eric found a Russian Tokarev TT-33, an old Soviet version of the Colt-Browning pistol. The eight-round magazine wasn't much, but the muzzle velocity surpassed the .45s. Ripping off the wet suit, he quickly put on the uniform and strapped the holster around his waist. Only then did he notice two more magazines lying in the bottom of the trunk. He quickly stuffed them in his pockets.

"You ready?" Simone asked.

With the black shawl covering her entire body and the *hijab* over her face, Simone had turned into any ordinary Iranian woman.

"You'll pass for one of their widows strolling down the street, but I'm not sure I'll satisfy inspection."

"Your time on the deck in the hot sun did its job. You don't realize how dark your face has become. A suntanned face makes you look like one of the locals. You'll do."

"Okay. How about a few clues on where we're going, Simone?"

Once again, she avoided looking directly at him. "We're not going into the town, but we'll take a dirt side road and hope to avoid the locals. We will walk slowly and quietly. Dogs will bark, but that is no problem. Once we're on the edge of the city, we will find a house that has already been prepared for us. There will be a computer inside. After we have entered, I will show you what comes next." She stopped and looked him squarely in the eyes. "Make sure your pistol is ready to fire at any given moment."

Eric pulled out the Tokarev TT-33 and cocked it. "I'll leave the chamber empty." He shoved it back into the holster. "It's been awhile since I've shot one of these Russian jobs, but I don't anticipate any problems. A little target practice would have been nice, though."

"Unfortunately, we can't afford such luxuries. Let's start walking." Simone shut the ramshackle door behind them.

In the moonlight, Eric could see the towering mountains silhouetted against the horizon. The air felt cool, soothing, far from the stifling heat of the Saudi Arabian desert. The Bandar skyline appeared small with almost no building over a couple of stories high. The winding dirt road remained quiet. Eventually, a goat herder came by guiding eight of his charges. Eric and Simone stepped aside and let him pass. No one spoke.

At points the dusty road almost became a path. Eventually a few flat-roofed houses appeared with candlelight shining through the windows. Dogs barked, but none approached them. Eric guessed they had walked at least four miles when more houses appeared.

Simone had said nothing, and Eric wondered what she must be thinking. All he could do was follow.

Without speaking, Simone pointed to her left and began cutting through a field covered with stubble. At the other end, she turned down what looked like an alley. After a hundred feet, she stopped in front of a stucco one-story flat-roofed house with a heavy padlock on the front door. Her hand reached out from under the drape hanging from her shoulders and stuck a key in the lock. It opened with a pinging sound.

"We have arrived," she said.

50

The battered door slowly opened with a squeaking noise. The sound sent a rat scurrying across the floor. A musty smell signaled no one had lived there for some time. Only a few dishes sat on exposed shelves along the wall. Dust covered the table in the center of the room.

Simone quickly lit a candle and set it in the center of the table. Saying nothing, she opened an old wooden cabinet standing next to the wall. Prying open a false back panel, she took out a laptop computer. From behind the cabinet, she pulled out a single telephone line with an attachment on the end.

"You may be surprised to learn that Benny Gantz set up this scenario. Benny does get around." Simone plugged the line into the back of the computer. "He knows Iran as if he grew up here. Took a little 'doing' to get this line wired in, but he accomplished the connection by running the line underground. Most of the people living around here pay little attention to anyone who looks like one of them. Their lives are simple, and they live from day to day trying to survive.

Not in their wildest dreams would they grasp what we are about to do." She turned on the computer.

"And what is it we are about to do?"

Simone watched the screen come up and remained silent. "Eric, it's not that I don't trust you. I hope you know that. But if we're captured, they'll torture you until you spill the truth. You might think you wouldn't do so, but eventually you would. Their methods are so cruel that eventually everyone surrenders. In order not to jeopardize our mission, I've told you as little as possible. I'm sorry if that makes it seem as if I don't trust you." She reached over, squeezed his hand, and looked deeply into his eyes for the first time in days. "I've done what I had to do."

She slung the black drape over her head and laid it across the table. She reached inside her shirt and pulled out the waterproof pouch from around her neck. She took out the USB device and pushed it into the computer.

"I've waited a long time for this moment," Simone said. "Everything now seems so simple. All I have to do is push a few buttons."

Intrigued, Eric watched her carefully.

Simone bent over the computer and began typing. In a few seconds, she was done.

"The worm's journey has begun," Simone said. "One big wreck is about to happen."

She closed her eyes and seemed to be mumbling a prayer. Her lips moved silently in an unceasing petition. Finally, she stopped and opened her eyes. Tears ran down her face.

"We've saved a countless number of lives."

"Really?"

Simone nodded. "Yes. I can again say no more until we are out of here. Believe me. Nothing your agency has ever done has been as important as this moment. We have stopped a monster. God will bless you for what you have done."

"And it's as simple as you plugging in the USB device and tapping in a few instructions?"

Simone smiled. "Well, we did have to sneak into Iran, but it is truly amazing, isn't it?"

"And we're done?"

"We are. I'll put this computer back, and we can return to the beach. We're on our way home." Simone reached out and squeezed his hand. "I can't tell you until later what has been accomplished, but you will be pleased. Now, we need to get out of here quickly. With their navy stationed in this town, eyes are everywhere."

"Get your widow's garb back on and let's hit the road." Eric paused to tap a message into his cell phone.

Job done. Going back to the tip of Qeshm Island.

Simone turned the computer off and stashed it back in the cabinet. Once again, she slung the drape over her head and blew the candle out.

"You ready?"

Eric peeked out the window. "Looks clear. I think we can leave without a problem."

"It may prove more difficult to get out than it did to get in," Simone said. "Regardless, we'll go back exactly as we came."

Eric pulled the gun from his holster and checked it again. "You'll be surprised at how fast I can fire." He snapped the holster shut. "By the way, once we get back on that island, how do we get out of here?"

Simone shrugged. "No problem. I anticipate an Israeli craft will find its way to us. Don't worry."

With total darkness hovering about them, they shut the door and Simone locked it. Once more, she started back down the alley. "We should be safe traveling the same path," she whispered. "Residents will look the other way if they see us. No one wants trouble."

"I'd buy a truckload of indifference right now," Eric said.

"We've got to get across that open field as quickly as possible. Once we're on the road, we'll be in a better position to go unnoticed."

He stepped up his pace, and they cut through the vacant lot quickly. Without slowing, they started down the road.

"Good," Simone whispered. "We'll get to the beach quickly now."

"Not too soon for me," Eric responded in a low, quiet voice. "I want out of here as fast as we can."

The winding road remained broader and more defined near the cluster of houses, but Eric knew it would soon narrow. Saying nothing, they walked slowly so as not to look in a hurry or draw attention.

Eric groaned. "Soldiers."

51

The AK-47 rifles dangled loosely from the three men's shoulders. Hard to tell in the dark, but they looked like regular enlisted men. Their casual demeanor differed from what Eric might have expected of a military unit. Then again, Iran always made a big show of the Revolutionary Guard while most of the other soldiers ran toward the shaggier side. The approaching patrol was walking on the down side of the hill. A significant dip in the road meant he and Simone would disappear before the soldiers came up again in front of them.

"If they speak, I'll answer," Simone said.

When the guards surfaced again, they instantly saluted Eric with a brisk sweep of their arms. Eric returned the salute but kept walking.

"Good to see you, sir," the first man said in Farsi. "We were not aware that officers would be here."

"He is a friend," Simone answered.

"I didn't ask you, woman," the soldier said with a sharp edge in his voice. "Speak only when you are spoken to."

Eric bristled. They weren't buying even an inch of Simone.

"You are rude," Simone blurted.

"Shut up, pig," a second soldier spouted, and raised his hand to hit her.

"Stop," Eric said.

The soldiers stiffened. "Where are you from?" the last man barked.

They hadn't figured it out yet, but the game was over. Eric reached for his gun before the men could react.

The first soldier dropped to his knees just as Eric shot him in the chest. The second grabbed his rifle from his shoulder, but Eric fired, sending him sprawling backward. Three shots whistled through the air before Eric shot the last man. The gun rolled from his hand, and the soldier fell forward.

"We have to get out of here fast," Eric said. "Run." He looked over at Simone. She lay hunched over on the ground.

"Simone?"

She groaned.

"You're hit!"

"Run," she demanded. "Get out of here."

"Where'd they shoot you?" Eric dropped down by her side and pulled the black hood back.

"A bullet in my thigh and one in my side." Simone pressed her hand a couple of inches above her waist. "I feel numb right now, but pain will set in quickly. Get out of here." Her eyes fluttered. "Leave me."

"I'm not leaving you!" Eric started to stand. "Got to get you on my back."

"No," Simone demanded. "I've completed my job. You get out of here. When other soldiers come, I'll fend them off . . . if I still can."

Eric grabbed her wrist tightly and pulled her forward. "I'm going to put you over my shoulder."

"No!"

"Don't struggle with me. You're heavy enough as it is."

"You can't carry me! They'll catch both of us."

"Then we'll go down together." He put his shoulder under her abdomen. "Your weight bearing down on my back will help cut off the bleeding. Your leg won't be a problem. I'll make some sort of a bandage when we reach the beach."

"You can't carry me that far. Leave me here. Please."

Eric pulled her over his shoulder, stood up, and grabbed her legs dangling in front of him. Clutching her as tightly as possible with his left arm, he hurried down the path. Simone kept groaning, and he could feel blood oozing onto his shirt. In the dim shadows, he could see the road turning back into a path. Rough terrain made it even more difficult to keep his footing and he feared tripping over rocks, but he kept grinding out the pace as fast as he could walk.

Training in the Colorado mountains had given him extra stamina at low altitude. His strong back kept her in a steady position, but they couldn't make good time. Eventually she would wear him down.

The path turned sharply and the trail disappeared in the shadows. Eric hadn't anticipated a quick turn. He tried to keep his feet on the path, but a root grabbed his foot and he tumbled forward. Simone moaned as she hit the ground.

"I'm sorry," Eric whispered in her ear. "I didn't—"

"Shh," she breathed. "Don't move."

Footfalls were coming toward them. Placing an arm under Simone's back and legs, he carried her to one side and laid her in a pile of brush. Spreading himself as flat as possible against the ground, he held the Tokarev in front of him and took aim.

He cocked the pistol.

The sound of whistling filled the night air. Eric raised his head for a better view. The goat herder they'd passed earlier had turned around and come back up the path. The noise of his eight goats sounded like a crowd tromping down the trail. Eric relaxed.

He crawled back to Simone. "We're safe," he said. "They're gone."

"Leave me here." Simone groaned. "I'm not going to make it. Leave me."

"Don't talk like that," Eric insisted. "You're going to make it. We're not that far from the beach."

"I'm too heavy and I'm bleeding. My leg's starting to throb."

"Listen to me," he insisted. "I'm taking you back to Qeshm Island if it's the last thing I do."

"It will be. You've got to leave me. I'll be dead by morning."

"Stop talking like a heroine in the movies. I'm going to pick you up again. Grit your teeth and hang on."

"No . . ." Her voice faded.

Eric carefully balanced her on his shoulder. Blood had run down his shirt, and his pants were stained. No time to worry about that. He had to move as fast as he could. He climbed back onto the trail and started toward the beach.

The moon slipped behind a cloud and the path became more difficult to see. Simone's breathing seemed to be more labored, and that worried him.

"You okay?" Eric asked.

No reply.

"You still with me?"

Again, no response.

Eric tried to trot, but the going was slow. He needed to rest again. Panting, he tried to breathe more deeply. No sounds were filtering down the path. No one had responded to the shooting.

Having caught his breath, he shifted Simone's body to the opposite shoulder, but she didn't move. Shock had set in. He needed to get her to the beach. Needed to keep moving. He slid her farther down his back and stood up.

The beach couldn't be too far away. The lane twisted and turned, but eventually the path became sandy. Eric knew they had to be close to the ocean. Somewhere in front of him, the sound of the surf echoed. When the moon reappeared, he saw the reflection of the ocean. The gentle lapping of the waves along the shore filled his ears with good news. All he needed to do was find that shack with their equipment inside. Simone had left her compass there and their wet suits as well. The stored goods were his ticket out of Iran. He dropped to one knee and laid her softly in the sand. She didn't move.

Eric started tapping a message that might go nowhere into his cell phone, but the attempt was all he could do at that moment.

SOS. Need help. On way to Qeshm Island. Emergency.

Would his message get out? Seemed doubtful. Then again, what else could he do? He clicked the phone off and picked up Simone again.

About 150 yards away, Eric recognized the dim outline of the old shack. Silhouetted against a bush-covered rise, the abandoned shanty looked like home. If nothing else, they could hide inside without fear of being seen. He trudged through the sand up the small hill. He kicked the door open and carried Simone inside, carefully lowering her to the floor. When he eased the shawl away from her body, he discovered that both bullets had gone completely through her. The amount of blood she'd lost was frightening, and the prospect of internal bleeding frightened him even more. All he could do was bandage the wounds to prevent any further hemorrhaging.

Eric lifted up the pieces of the floor and set them against the wall. He tore off his shirt and ripped the back side into long strips. With his pocketknife, he cut the leg off Simone's pants and began packing the wound. As rapidly as possible, he tied one of the strips around the bullet wound. The bandage seemed tight enough to hold but not to stop circulation in the rest of her leg. With the rest of the bloody shirt, he put a compress against her back and side.

"What are you doing?" Simone moaned.

"I'm trying to make sure your wounds don't bleed while we swim back to the island."

"I can't swim. I'm not even sure that I can move my leg anymore. There could be sharks in the ocean."

"Yeah. I know. We'll have to chance it. We can't get caught here. Don't worry. I'm your motorboat."

"You can't get me across. Save yourself. Leave me here." Her voice began to fade.

Eric kept adjusting the compress. Simone's eyes closed, and he knew she was out. Putting the wet suit back on her wouldn't be easy, but the temperatures dropped sharply at night, and he couldn't chance her physical condition being worsened by being in the water.

Eric pulled the suit over Simone's legs and up her body. Once he got the suit up to her waist, he took a couple of pieces of the flooring and made a splint that kept her knee from bending. If nothing else, bleeding would not be aggravated during their swim. Simone offered no resistance when he slipped the rest of the suit around her. Oxygen would be important, and the mask would keep the ocean from drowning her. Simone might revive in the sea, but then again, she might not. He had to be prepared for her total dependency on him.

He put on his wet suit, knowing he'd have to carry the oxygen tanks down to the beach and come back for Simone and the fins. He put on Simone's compass wristwatch and started down with a container in each hand.

The smell of the ocean filled his nose, and the sand oozed up between his toes. A drop in temperature felt refreshing as the breeze blew against his face, but the suit warmed up quickly while lugging the heavy oxygen tanks. Eric spotted a large tree stump sticking up out of the sand that could provide a good hiding place for the tanks. Only then did he realize two men were crouched down in the sand only thirty feet from him.

Eric watched the dark shapes creeping toward him. They didn't look like soldiers and were probably marauders slinking along the beach looking for easy pickings. What he could see of their clothing suggested they were average types that might be strolling through any Iranian town. A lone man in a wet suit had to appear as an easy target. He had to act naturally then smack the first guy with an oxygen tank. The rest shouldn't be much of a problem.

The sound of men running across the beach signaled the assault was on. Eric bent over slightly with his back toward them and didn't move. The first man screamed and leaped through the air. With all his might, Eric whacked him with the oxygen tank. The assailant hit the beach like a piece of driftwood. The other man abruptly stopped and looked shocked. Turning quickly, he started running in the opposite direction.

A high-pitched squealing sound came from the sand. He looked down and to his shock discovered the valve on the top of the oxygen tank had bent in the struggle. Pressurized gas had started spewing out. Eric grabbed the tank and examined it more closely. The blow had slightly bent the nozzle, rendering the entire supply useless. No longer could they both use oxygen to cross the strait. The other tank would have to go to Simone, and he'd need to swim with nothing on but a snorkel.

Eric dropped to his knees and began tying the attacker's hands behind his back, using the man's belt to hold him steady, but his mind raced through the alternatives. Could he swim the distance pulling an unconscious Simone behind him? If the ocean got rough, would the waves choke him and force him to let go of her? She'd sink like a weight, and in the darkness he'd never find her. A grim sense of reality swept over him. Rather than escaping, they might be heading into disaster.

52

The salty smell of seawater settled around them as the tide raced in. Eric laid Simone down on the beach to finalize his preparations. Not far away, the attacker lay in the sand, securely bound and not moving. A glance told Eric the mugger wouldn't be wiggling for a long time. The oxygen tank probably took out plenty of his teeth. The side of his jaw had already begun to swell.

After fastening the oxygen tank on Simone's back, he pulled the diving mask over her nose and mouth. Carefully, slowly, he adjusted the tension to make sure nothing leaked and that it wouldn't be too tight. Several times she groaned but nothing more. Finally he turned on the oxygen. Putting his face close to hers, he made sure she kept breathing normally.

Could he make the swim? Normally, it would be no question, but pulling another person behind him with a heavy tank on her back amounted to an almost Herculean task. The wind had picked up and the waves looked choppy, which only increased the strain. If his arm slipped and he lost control, she'd easily disappear beneath the waves. Eric didn't scare easily, but fear crept up his spine. No matter what happened, he couldn't lose Simone.

The moon slipped out from behind the passing clouds and highlighted the beach. He looked down at this delicate woman sprawled in the sand and feared the loss of blood might take her life before the ocean could. No matter how testy their exchanges had been on the freighter, he couldn't deny his feelings. If he couldn't swim with her in tow to the island, then he'd die with her beneath the waves. No halfway attempts on this night. They'd make it together or not at all.

Bowing on his knees in the sand, Eric closed his eyes. *Heavenly Father, you know that I'd give my life for this woman. In fact, if you want to take me instead, I'll go with the flow. Please, please, don't let her die out there in the ocean. I need you to give me the strength to get back to that island. Please put a little extra gas in my tank and keep my motor running. I'd be forever grateful. Okay? Amen.* After a deep breath, he stood up.

Eric slipped on his fins and tugged Simone away from the shore. Slipping his arm across her chest and under her body, he assumed the lifesaver position he'd learned many years ago. Drawing his legs up under his body, he kicked out and pushed away. Slowly, they edged out into the Strait of Hormuz. The sandy bottom disappeared quickly, and Eric knew he had entered the deep. No stopping now.

The waves lifted him and bounced them around like children's toys, but he kept pushing. Periodically, the waves splashed against his face, and he coughed to flush the saltwater out. Simone's stillness worried him. But there was nothing he could do but keep swimming. Eric pumped his legs and kept his free hand paddling. Each time his arm came back, he glanced at the compass wristwatch to make sure he maintained his direction. The first kilometer wouldn't be the problem; the danger was in what would follow.

As he felt his strength ebbing, Eric realized he needed to get his mind off how he felt. He had to think of some memory, some idea, some need that would keep him from succumbing to fatigue.

He remembered his childhood swimming teacher, a guy named Mel Bates.

After one of the lessons, Mel had called him aside. "Son, you're a fine athlete. Sometimes you have to grit your teeth and learn how to tough it out. Endurance is everything."

Eric had looked up at Mel's face, unsure of what he meant. "Endurance?"

"Endurance is in your head, not your body." Mel smiled. "It's a mental deal. Endurance is fastening your mind on the objective and not letting anything deter you." He slapped Eric on the back. "Got it, kid?"

Eric just stared at him.

"That's the secret. Learn to keep your eye on one target and not be distracted by the flack flying around you."

A huge wave crashed over Eric, and the memory faded. Clutching Simone even more tightly, he clamped his mouth shut and waited for the ocean to settle. The next surge lifted both of them back up again, and the swell pushed him along. "Endurance is in the mind," Mel had said. He had to remember that lesson and keep his mind locked on one objective. Somewhere Qeshm Island waited for them.

53

The force of the ocean waves bounced Eric's head up and down while he fought not to sink beneath the waves. Several times he thought he might drown, but his steady leg kicks brought him up again. Simone's body floated still, but he hung on for dear life. When she seemed to be slipping away from him, he shifted her to the other side of his body.

Simone had told him that an Israeli watercraft would swing into the shore, but how would he know to make contact? When? Where? Simone couldn't tell him if she remained unconscious. The longer she was out, the greater the chance that she'd never wake up. He was caught in a catch-22 with no options. If the Israelis didn't show, somebody from that island would find them. By then, everyone would know about the shooting in Bandar. The Iranians would pounce on them like lions on fresh meat.

When a strong wave lifted him up again, he caught sight of the faint outline of the island. The moon highlighted the irregular shape of terrain framed against the black horizon. Was there another island out there? He hoped not. Eric didn't know if he could get to the shore, but he kept pressing on.

Mel Bates had told him endurance was in his head. The idea sounded good in a swimming pool locker room. With his arms limp from fatigue and legs about to give out, the inspiration had vanished. If he quit, they'd both sink, and soldiers would never have a shot at them. Not a bad idea.

Would Simone quit if their situations were reversed?

She wouldn't. Her motto had been to fight to the death. Keep going. Don't stop. Kick. Swim. He had to keep going until it was impossible to do otherwise, if for no other reason than for Simone's sake.

His legs felt like lead and his arms had turned to putty. Closing his eyes, he pushed ahead, fearing he would soon lose control and sink to the bottom. His body had begun to shut down. His senses seemed to be fading, and he felt numb. The battle wouldn't go on much longer. His thoughts scrambled and became incoherent. His body was going down.

Something touched his fins. How could that be? Eric pulled his feet over what must be a rock. How could a rock be out in the middle of the ocean? Didn't feel like a rock. Felt more like sand. The fins seemed to be gliding on a solid surface, but that couldn't be. He was sinking in the sea. His knees buckled and settled into the sandy bottom. Only then did he look straight ahead. Waves were breaking on a beach. Tall trees stood behind a long stretch of sand. Eric pulled Simone up on the shore and fell beside her. Crawling on his knees, he tugged her further up on the sand before he collapsed.

⟡⟡⟡

When Eric awoke, the blackness of a dark night had settled over them. His mind began to clear. For the first time, he fully realized that he had made it to Qeshm Island. His legs might cramp and his arms felt numb, but he needed to get the wet suit off. Peeling the rubber covering from his body proved to be a task, but he got the suit pulled down to his legs and finally stepped away.

For a moment, he studied Simone. If he pulled her suit off, it might cause her wounds to start hemorrhaging. Best leave the wet suit alone. Eric pulled the mask away from her eyes and took the regulator from her mouth. With a sense of dread, he lowered his head near her mouth and nose, hoping against hope that she might still be breathing. With a huge sigh of relief, he rocked back on his heels. She had survived the crossing.

Simone had endured. Maybe she could make it through the rest of the journey. Bowing his head, he prayed. *You saved us. Thank you. Thank you. Thank you . . .*

Eric's prayer faded away. He bent over with his head nearly touching the white sandy beach. Finally, he sat up again and leaned back on his haunches. Eric had no idea what kind of network of communication the Iranian military might have. Usually, the equipment in the backwoods was pitifully spartan. Then again, because the navy maintained such a strong presence in Bandar, they'd probably hit the alarm button. Would they also search the distant shoreline of Qeshm Island? Yeah, they would. Once again, he felt the icy reality that there was nowhere to hide.

A sound in the distance caught his attention. He listened intently. A thumping beat filled the sky. The noise sounded like helicopter blades beating the air. He didn't need a second look. A large helicopter was coming straight toward them.

54

The steady beat of helicopter blades grew louder as the shape of an approaching chopper became more evident. A beam of light swept across the treetops, searching, probing, pushing relentlessly forward. The helicopter had to be searching for them. Eric found himself with an impossible dilemma. If he tried to carry Simone into the trees behind the beach, they'd spot him running across the sand. The enemy would wipe them out before he got halfway. Moving Simone was out of the question. Not moving meant being seen immediately. The blackness of night certainly wouldn't hide them from the searchlight.

Eric pulled the pistol from his belt. A pistol wouldn't do much good against a fully armed military chopper, but it was his only defense. Eric studied Simone sprawled on the beach. Her black wet suit might look like a rock if her legs were partially buried in the sand and her arms pushed against her body. If he laid over her and pulled his wet suit across both of them, a fast-moving chopper might think they were only debris. It was a long shot but the only one that he had.

Digging furiously with his hands, Eric carved out a hole

and pushed the sand to one side. The chopper's noise increased. The crew was scouring every inch of the beach. He pushed Simone's feet and part of her shins into the small hole and frantically heaped the sand over them, hopefully leaving the right appearance of an elongated black rock. If he covered her with his body, he just might pull off the right appearance and they'd be off the hook.

"Oh, Lord, we're not out of the forest yet," he prayed aloud. "Hate to bother you again so soon, but if those soldiers shoot, we're dead. Please, please, help us look obscure. Amen."

The helicopter veered to the right and swooped back across the tree-covered island. Eric couldn't believe his prayer had been that effective. He started to breathe again. Maybe the soldiers were going to search in another area.

The chopper slowed and hovered above the trees. A searchlight kept sweeping across the mass of brush lining the beach. The helicopter stopped. After a minute, the craft started moving again. Coming in their direction.

Eric doubled over Simone again and held her close. "I'm sorry," he moaned. "So sorry. I'm afraid they're coming for us."

The bright beam broke through the tree line, methodically searching the brush and small scrubs along the edge of the beach. The piercing light edged toward the ocean. Eric ducked his head and squeezed Simone close to his chest. She didn't move. He clenched his eyes. The roar of the motor became deafening, growling like an angry dragon devouring everything in its path.

The chopper lowered; the thumping increased. They had spotted him. In a matter of seconds, the attackers would be all over the beach. Whether they survived or not would depend on how many soldiers were in the chopper. He could prob-ably stop four of them before they got him. More than that, and it would be over.

The helicopter hovered above them and then swung slightly to the left. Sand started blowing as the craft lowered to the beach. The speed of the large blades decreased; the noise remained deafening.

Eric reasoned that when the soldiers rushed out, he would leap up and run away from Simone. She'd be less vulnerable if he drew their fire. He could dive into the sand and fire as the soldiers approached. He hunkered down.

The side door of the helicopter slid open. The motor shut off. The noise of the blades diminished. A man stepped out. Eric could get him immediately. He slowly raised the pistol and aimed. Easy target.

"Eric!"

How could some Iranian know his name?

"Eric? Is that you?"

The voice sounded strangely familiar.

"Eric, it's me."

Eric aimed at the soldier running toward him. His mind must be playing tricks on him. He put his finger on the trigger.

"It's me!" the man yelled again. "Jack Javidi!"

Eric caught his breath.

"We're going to get you out of here."

Another figure jumped out of the helicopter. "We found you!" a woman's voice echoed across the beach. "We've done it!"

Eric lowered the gun. He knew that voice well. "How'd you find us?"

"I picked up your SOS," Jack said.

"But how'd you get here so quickly?"

"I've been in Iraq for several weeks," Jack explained. "George believed that would be a good location if you got into trouble. I started monitoring your calls from Baghdad and then flew south when your distress signal came in."

The woman in military fatigues dropped in the sand beside Eric.

"Sarah?" Eric swallowed hard. "It's really you?"

"I'm sorry I didn't dress for the occasion." Sarah grinned. "This was all I could scratch up in Baghdad. Not my usual style. I flew over when we found out where you were going."

"How'd you get past Iranian security?"

"This chopper's marked as one of theirs. Listen, Eric. We've got to get you out of here. How bad is Simone hurt?"

"She got shot twice and needs immediate medical attention."

"Sarah, get the stretcher." Jack pointed back toward the helicopter. "We'll secure her inside the craft. Then we're out of here. We'll fly low getting off the island. All we have to do is get back across the strait and we're home free. Iraq's just on the other side of the pond."

Sarah ran up with the stretcher. "I'll slide the canvas under her while you guys lift her up."

"Don't bend her leg," Eric said. "She's got a wound in her thigh."

"Easy does it," Jack said. "Get it completely under her, Sarah."

The two men grabbed the handles and hustled back to the chopper.

Sarah jumped in. "We've got emergency equipment inside.

An IV came with the emergency medical supplies." Sarah inserted the needle into Simone's arm and secured her to the back of the craft. "We're ready," Sarah said. "Fire it up, Jack."

The blades began turning. "Put that helmet on, Eric," Jack said. "It's got earphones inside." The engine revved up. The chopper began to lift.

Eric watched the island grow smaller while the helicopter turned out toward the ocean. The sea appeared calm and quiet. Far off in the distance, he could see the lights of a large city glowing in the night. Against the steady beat of the blades, the night appeared still and peaceful. He watched freighters making their way down the strait toward ports along the edge of the land. No one appeared to be paying attention to a lone helicopter flying across the sea. For the first time, Eric realized that his prayers had been answered beyond any possibility that he could have dreamed. They were safe.

Thank you, Lord, Eric prayed silently. *Thank you more than I can possibly say.*

"When we get inside Iraq," Jack said over the audio system, "we'll land and refuel. Once we're gassed up, we'll fly straight toward Baghdad. Inside the Green Zone, we can get the medical attention Simone needs. We've got good doctors working in their hospital. She'll be okay."

Eric watched the moon's reflection in the waves gently rolling beneath them. Good doctors in Baghdad?

He prayed so.

55

The lights of Baghdad sparkled like a thousand candles against the night sky. In contrast to the small villages that were now dark, the city appeared to seldom sleep. With the moon shining brightly over the sand, Eric caught fleeting glimpses of the barren desert beneath them. The warfare that had constantly swept through Iraq left tanks and the debris of war scattered over the flat terrain. He could see only one highway that moved in a relentlessly straight line from wherever on to the capital city.

"Not much to see down there," Jack spoke into the microphone attached to his helmet.

"Yeah," Eric answered into his headset. "Looks bleak."

"And dangerous. I'm going to fly higher in case some local wants to take a little target practice." The helicopter started to lift.

"Fighting still going on?"

Jack nodded. "Always will be. Sunnis and the Shiites don't ever seem to call a truce. The Iraqi government sits on a powder keg that could go off any time. Got to keep your eyes open."

Eric looked over his shoulder and shouted to Sarah. "How's Simone doing?"

Sarah shrugged. "Can't say." Sarah's voice barely exceeded the noise of the helicopter engine.

"Can we go any faster?" Eric asked.

"I got it on full throttle. Don't worry, we're making good time."

Eric watched the back of the chopper. Sarah kept monitoring Simone's vital signs carefully. He couldn't ask for any better attention. It was simply that they needed to get her to a hospital immediately.

Leaning back in his seat, Eric watched the landscape again. The edge of the city came into view, and he knew they'd be at the hospital soon. Not many cars out on the streets at three in the morning. Baghdad seemed reasonably quiet.

"Flying in with a patient," Jack said into the microphone. "I'll land in the Green Zone. We need a doctor on standby." The helicopter immediately dropped closer to the rooftops.

"Roger," a voice echoed through the headset. "Pay close attention. There's been unrest this evening."

"Got ya," Jack answered. "Thanks for the heads-up."

"What's he mean?" Eric asked.

"Sounds like a remnant of al-Qaeda might be hanging around. We've got a number of terrorists roaming. They're out there."

"Sure," Eric said. "That's the information I was picking up before I started off on this expedition. Mad dogs are still running loose."

"Hang on," Jack said. "But don't worry. We're about there."

The chopper kept humming through the night. Eric took a deep breath and relaxed.

The sounds of a rifle cracked through the darkness.

"Shooting at us?" Eric frantically reached to hang on.

Another much louder blast rocked the helicopter.

"These boys aren't kidding," Jack said. "Got to get up higher."

The window next to Eric exploded, and a piece of the windshield in front of him shattered and went flying away. The motor started missing and the thumping became irregular.

"We're hit!" Jack shouted. "Hang on. We've got to get to the Green Zone."

The chopper kept dropping and swinging wildly to the left.

"Mayday! Mayday!" Jack shouted into the microphone. "We've been hit. On the edge of the city. Dropping fast."

Eric couldn't make out the radio response because of the garbled sound, but the sudden drop in altitude put his stomach in his mouth. Eric grabbed a handhold to steady himself.

The craft kept swinging to the left, and the motor's irregularity signaled the chopper could drop at any minute.

"They must have hit a rotor," Jack yelled. "Might have put a hole in a stabilizer. Can't tell. Hope we can get down before the motor quits."

Eric tightened his grip and clutched the handhold like he might tear it off. The continual rapid descent of the craft left him light-headed and terrified. He looked over his shoulder to see if Simone had moved. The belts had held her in place. Sarah clung to the stretcher unit like her life depended on it.

Flat rooftops were coming up quickly. Telephone lines weren't far below them. He could see an alley, a street rising up toward them at breakneck speed. Couldn't be fifty feet below them. The helicopter kept veering to the left. Suddenly, the irregular sputtering of the motor stopped and the thumping of the blades became regular. The craft still veered, but the descent had become regular.

Eric caught his breath. Maybe they could land without a problem.

"Oh no!" Jack shouted. "The motor stopped!"

The chopper dropped like a chunk of lead thrown in a pond. A crashing noise exploded with the sound of timber tearing apart. The bottom of the chopper pushed upward, jamming Eric's legs up toward his chest. For a moment, his lungs deflated. His head smacked against the side of the door, but the helmet stayed secure. In the dim light pouring in from the hole in the roof above them, Eric could see a large room. They had smashed through a roof into a warehouse filled with building supplies. Felt like the helicopter had landed on a stack of cement bags.

"You okay?" Jack asked.

"Think so," Eric said. "What happened?"

"The motor started to fly right, and then it just stopped."

"Sarah!" Eric yelled. "How are you back there?"

"I've had easier landings," she said with the usual ironic twist in her voice. "Maybe next time we can hire a real pilot."

"Simone?" Eric shouted.

"I think being strapped on a stretcher did the trick. She's no worse."

"We've got to get out of here," Jack said. "The radio's out and the word will quickly spread that we're down. No telling what they'll try to throw at us."

Eric released the seat belt and crawled out. "The two of you can carry Simone. I'll cover you."

"Let's get moving." Jack pushed his way out of the seat and climbed into the back. "We need to get out of this dump now."

"Looks like the crash broke the sliding door open," Eric observed. "We can get her out without a problem." He could hear people talking somewhere outside the building. "Let's hurry."

While Sarah and Jack maneuvered Simone out of the craft, Eric looked for a front door. He finally found an old rusted metal door locked on the outside. No way to break through except to force it open. He couldn't smash through the barrier without sounding like the Fifth Army on the march. No alternative.

Eric rushed at the door and threw his weight against it. The sound of the lock tearing out of the doorjamb cracked with a ripping thump. The door tore off the hinges and smashed into the pavement. Eric tumbled out on top of the tin sheets.

A small crowd had gathered on the other side of the alley and stood pointing at the building. Eric stared at them, unsure of what would come next. One of the women screamed, and the rest instantly dispersed.

For a moment, Eric laid on the dilapidated door, wondering if some hidden figure had a gun aimed at him. "Get Simone out here!" he shouted back into the warehouse. "Now!"

Jack quickly walked out holding the stretcher behind him with Sarah bringing up the rear. Jack nodded to the right. "Don't stop."

They darted up the dark passageway while lights started to go on. People were waking up to the fact that something had happened in their neighborhood. Eric turned the corner and led them along a sidewalk bordering a street where a streetlight illuminated the area. Eric knew it wasn't good to be out in the light, but at least they were out of that alley.

At the corner of a wide boulevard, Eric dropped to his knees and turned to Jack. "I have no idea which way to go. You've been here before. Got any ideas?"

Jack shook his head.

"Me, neither," Sarah said. "But I've got a cell phone, though I don't know if it'll work. Think we can connect with a command center?"

"Let's try," Jack said. "I've got a couple of numbers that I keep with me in case of an emergency. One of them might work."

Sarah handed him the phone.

Jack dialed the number and was silent for a moment. "This is Jack Javidi. I'm an American with two other Americans and a wounded Israeli woman. We were in a helicopter, and we crashed through the roof of a warehouse. We're caught here on the corner of Walk and Don't Walk with Iraqis shooting at us." He was quiet a moment. "We've been flying in from the south and are on the edge of the city near Salah Ed Din street. Radar picked us up coming in. You can get a location from them. We're just around the corner on the main street from where we crashed."

Eric listened but kept watching the roof of the building across the street where he thought he saw movement along the roofline. A sniper could be lurking up there.

"Got it!" Jack said in the phone. "If you boys linger, you'll find our bodies out here on the boulevard next to the streetlight." He hung up.

"Think they'll get here?" Eric asked.

Jack shook his head. "I don't think so. Not in time to bail us out of this mess alive."

"There's movement on the top of that building over there." Eric pointed across the street.

"Yeah," Sarah said. "Look. With these army fatigues, they'll think I'm male. The cap covers my hair. That makes three men aiming at them." She pulled her Walther PPK pistol out of her belt and cocked it. "We're all excellent shots. We can take them on."

Simone groaned and slightly raised her hand.

"She's moving," Sarah said. "That won't help."

"Let's carry Simone back against that doorway over there," Eric said. "Then each of us can lie flat on the cement and prepare for whoever comes next."

"Good idea," Jack said. "I think that's the best approach. Whether the army shows up or not, we're covered."

Simone moaned when they placed her next to a ramshackle door. "I hope she's not coming around. I gave her a sedative during the flight, but that might be fading," Sarah said.

"We've done the best we can do," Jack said. "Let's get hunkered down."

Eric patted her hand. "Hang in there, Simone."

She didn't move.

"Okay," Eric said. "Try to stay covered as best you can. Pull your military caps down tight."

They positioned themselves to cover both the street and the roof. Eric saw movement once more along the top of the building. "Looks like there might be two of them scurrying back and forth. If they had a night scope, they'd have an easy time hitting us. Those dirtbags probably don't have such sophisticated equipment." He aimed his pistol straight in front of him.

"They might be street sweepers simply watching from the roof," Sarah whispered. "We don't know that they're assassins."

"Let's hope we're watching prowlers out for a late-night burglary," Jack said. "Could be."

A head popped up above the bricks and seemed to be looking right at them. Eric steadied his gun. The figure dropped down again. Eric looked at his watch. Time was ticking away. "The longer we're out here, the more vulnerable we become," he said. "This can't go on forever."

"Yeah," Jack answered. "We're going to find out how efficient the army is."

"I'm not sure those moving heads are our original shooters," Sarah whispered again.

"Might not be," Jack said.

The crack of a rifle shattered the front window beside them. Eric fired back instantly. Glass sprayed over the street and flew past their heads. Jack fired. No one moved on the roof.

"Answers that question," Sarah said. "The yardbirds are definitely out tonight. Get ready."

Simone's weak voice floated from behind them. "W-where am I?"

Eric hustled back and grabbed her hand. "We're in Baghdad. You're on the way to the hospital."

"Hospital?" Simone sounded weak but coherent.

"Don't worry," Eric said.

"Hospital?" Her voice faded away.

"Two return shots may have given them pause to reconsider," Jack said. "These bush-league boys are hit-and-run specialists. Could be gone by now."

"Wouldn't count on it," Sarah said. "Keep your heads down."

The hum of a motor pierced the night air. Eric listened again. Sounded like some sort of vehicle zooming down the street. Maybe a truckload of their cousins with heavy artillery had been called in. They'd stand no chance against such an adversary.

"Hear that truck?" he asked. "We may have some unwelcome company."

Sarah said nothing but pushed more closely toward the wall where the large plate-glass window had been shot out.

With the increasing brightness of the headlights flying toward them, Eric had no doubt these guys meant business.

The vehicle came to a screeching halt in front of them. Six men poured out of the back of the American army troop carrier. One soldier aimed an automatic weapon at the roofline and fired a round of bullets that would have terrified the dead.

"You called?" a soldier asked, running up to them.

"You got here fast," Jack said. "We've got a wounded woman back there on a stretcher."

"We'll get her and haul you out of here." The soldier snapped his fingers. Two men trotted over.

"Okay," the soldier continued. "We'll put the three of you in the back of the carrier. Our men will stay around for a while policing the area. Get in and let's go."

Within seconds, the stretcher had been secured. Eric's team

found seats, and the armored vehicle raced away. No one spoke for a number of blocks.

Eric turned to Jack. "About that helicopter. The army won't be happy with a damaged chopper. We're liable."

"No problem."

"What do you mean?"

"No one will have anything to say." Jack grinned.

"I'm missing something here. Where'd you get it?"

"I borrowed it. No one's going to be looking for us."

Eric blinked several times. "People generally don't lend military helicopters. Where'd you pick that one up?"

"I borrowed it from the Iraqi military."

56

The military troop carrier bounced along Baghdad's streets, swinging from right to left to avoid huge potholes. The foul odor from the alley no longer hung in the air; the scent of grease and tires smelled good for a change. The heavily armored vehicle felt as if it were moving at top speed, and Eric certainly hoped the driver was paying close attention. With such high rpms, they could probably plow through a brick building without slowing. He felt confident the soldiers knew what they were doing. Still, he worried that a collision would further injure Simone. Moreover, street bombs were still a threat. Insurgents would love to hit a troop carrier in the early morning hours. He settled back against the side of the carrier and uttered another prayer for their safety.

After a silent "amen," he thought about the past months. Years ago, his personal faith had shifted from the church to believing in the highest American ideals. Defending the nation became his ultimate form of worship. On this cold night in a city that dated back to biblical times, he realized another shift had occurred in his thinking. Simone's steadfast faith in the God of Abraham, Isaac, and Jacob had impressed him more than he had realized. After all, he believed in the same God. Behind his patriotic convictions stood an even more absolute truth. Simone had been willing to give her life for Israel, but that was because Israel was an extension of her faith. His belief in America amounted to the same thing. What counted most were the convictions that stood behind and inspired those noble dreams. Struggling to survive their recent battles, he had peered behind his sense of patriotism to find more basic principles and convictions. In this crisis, he had not prayed to the White House, the Washington Monument, or the Constitution. His prayers had gone up to the Almighty, and God had answered him. The hand of God had saved them from disaster.

Simone had extraordinary skill with a weapon, but what had stopped them from being assassinated in London? What kept him alive in Stuttgart, Germany? How had Simone missed getting blown up in her house in Washington DC? Eric stayed in top physical condition and could thread a needle with a bullet, but other excellent marksmen had died with one crack of a rifle. He and Simone had wound their way through a rattlesnake den without one fatal bite. Only the unseen hand of God could have sustained them through such a perilous journey.

His commitment hadn't been wrong; he just hadn't aimed high enough. What greater evidence could there be than that, in a matter of hours, he and Simone had gone from certain death at the hands of enemy soldiers to riding down main street in an armored car. She was alive and by God's grace would survive. How could such a remarkable escape have occurred? Only by the provision that came from the hand of God.

No matter what the future might hold for Simone and him, he knew he had changed. He didn't have to back away from his fierce commitment to the American dream, but his ultimate allegiance belonged to God.

"We're almost there," a man's voice echoed over the vehicle's inner loudspeaker. "I'm going to pull into a military hospital in a few moments."

"Thank God!" Sarah said. "I thought we'd never get across this city!"

Jack smiled. "I don't know about you, but I'm ready for some old-fashioned shut-eye."

"Me too." Sarah yawned.

Eric's body ached from exhaustion, and he knew he could fall asleep instantly, but he had to know Simone was in surgery before he drifted away.

The vehicle slowed. Red and white lights flashed outside. The carrier came to a halt. Some guy yanked the back door open.

"Get out of the way," a voice yelled. Uniformed men appeared, wheeling a gurney.

"Where's she hit?" The soldier pointed at Simone.

"Got shot in the thigh and the side," Eric said. "Hurry!"

The soldiers pulled Simone's stretcher out and placed her on the gurney. A doctor in scrubs stood at the door. Grabbing the side of the cart, he and the men rushed her through the swinging door and down the hall.

"Is there a room where we can lie down?" Eric asked. "It feels like we've been flying forever."

"Sure. Follow me."

Eric fell in beside the officer. The antiseptic smell of the hospital filled his nose with a refreshing scent. "Got any idea how long surgery will take?"

"Can't say. However, they'll have her in a room and awake before you're able to visit. I'd suggest the three of you get some rest. Don't worry. We're going to take good care of your friend."

"Thank you."

The officer turned a corner and pointed to a small room just off the hallway. "You'll find some blankets in there. We'll come for you when it's time to see her."

Eric walked into the dim room, feeling like he could sleep on a rock. Sarah grabbed a blanket, lay down, and was gone.

Eric lay down on the cot and took a deep breath.

"I want you to know that we're proud of you," Jack said to him. "You risked your life and won the battle. I'm honored to work for you, partner."

"Thanks," Eric mumbled.

He stretched out and realized how grateful he was. Staring up at the white ceiling, he envisioned a star-filled night sky hovering above him. *Thank you*, he prayed. In seconds, he was asleep.

57

The faint light of early morning settled over Tehran. Only the slight noise of a few automobiles echoed down the streets when the door to Ayatollah Ali Hashemi's bedroom cracked slightly. His closest aide peered into the darkness but knew he must not stop. Pushing the door open, he stepped in.

"Sir," the aide called out in a loud voice. "Sorry. You must wake up."

"W-what?" the Supreme Leader mumbled.

"An important matter awaits your attention, sir."

The ayatollah pushed himself up in bed. "Is it morning?"

"Almost, sir. Unfortunately, President Ebrahim Jalili awaits you downstairs."

"Jalili!" the mullah bellowed. "I hate to be awakened early."

"I know, sir. However, the president said his visit is urgent."

"What does that idiot want?"

"I do not know. He only stressed that he must speak with you privately."

"Tell him I'll be down when I am dressed." The mullah swung his skinny legs out of the bed. "Go on."

The aide bowed and hurried away.

❖-❖-❖

The Supreme Leader walked into the library with a scowl on his face. He nodded to Jalili but said nothing.

"I apologize, sir. Unfortunately, I have information that we must discuss immediately."

Ayatollah Ali Hashemi pointed to a chair. "Sit down." He pulled a larger gold inlaid chair closer.

"I immediately came here after I received the report from our office that oversees our nuclear centrifuges at the Fordow facility. We have sustained severe damage that our engineers do not believe is an accident."

The ayatollah bolted forward. "What do you mean?"

Jalili said, "The incident has to do with the operation of our centrifuges. At a high speed of rotation, gas is compressed close to the wall of the rotor. The rotor can be almost a meter in length with a temperature gradient of three hundred centrigrade between the top and bottom of the rotor. Of course, this produces a strong convection current. In addition, very strong force produces added separation efficiency."

"Yes, yes," Hashemi said. "Spare me the technical details. Get on with it."

"To put it bluntly, someone hacked into one of the contractors that worked on the centrifuges. In turn, they gained access to our 984 new centrifuges."

"Yes, yes. Go on."

"The hackers accomplished a remarkable achievement. The frequency converters keep the motors running at 1,007 cycles per second. However, these foreign invaders have caused the motors to run wild while the monitors indicated nothing, resulting in the destruction of our centrifuges. We have suffered a major setback."

The ayatollah's mouth dropped. "Destroyed?" he repeated in almost a whisper. "Who did this?"

"The investigation has just begun. We are struggling to understand exactly how they got through the firewalls that protect our facility. We suspect they carried this out from inside Iran. It is too early for us to track down all the intricacies of such a system. However, one of our systems analysts has come up with a clue."

The ayatollah pressed forward. "What is it?"

"Like leaving a calling card behind, they left the word *myrtus*. Our analyst believes the name refers to Hadassah, the birth name of Queen Esther, the Jewish woman who saved the Jews from our ancestors in Persia."

58

A freight train flying out of the blackness careened toward Eric while he fought to free his foot from between the steel rails. No matter how hard he jerked, he couldn't work his foot loose. Eric screamed. The train smashed into him. When he emerged out of a cloudy fog, a giant vulture stood only feet away, eyeing him like prime roadkill. Almost four feet tall, the ugly bird studied him with bloodshot eyes and razor-sharp talons. The bird began walking slowly around him, relentlessly stalking him with gruesome eyes. Eric started backing away; the bird kept coming. He reached for his gun; it was gone. The vulture raised its awesome wings and beat the air before creeping straight toward him. He had no defense.

"Eric." A hand shook him. "Wake up!"

Sunlight beamed through the window. He shielded his eyes.

"Time to get up."

Eric peered into the face of a soldier bending over him.

"You've been asleep for nearly eight hours," the soldier said. "It's late morning."

Eric sat up and rubbed his eyes. "Morning? How could it . . ."

"You needed the sleep after yesterday's roller-coaster ride."

"Yesterday?" Eric ran his hands through his hair. "Yesterday!" He sprang to his feet. "Simone! How's Simone?"

"If you'll come with me, you can see her now."

Eric looked at his rumpled clothes. He had changed into old khakis found in a back room when they refueled in Iraq, but that had been hours ago. A day ago. At least the wet suit had been left behind. He rubbed his face and felt the stubble on his chin. "I don't look too swift."

"Around here, we're happy when patients come in with clothing still on them. We see far too many with their clothes blown off. You look fine." The soldier ushered him down the hall.

"You been here long?"

"It's my second tour," the soldier said.

"How's Simone?"

"She's lost a considerable amount of blood, but the leg wound didn't give us any problems. We transfused her with two pints of blood, and that helped. Unfortunately, the wound in her side turned out to be more serious. Surgery was required, but no vital organs were hit. She's been asleep, but she's coming around now. She's been calling for you when she's alert."

Eric took a deep breath. "Very good."

The soldier pointed ahead. "This is our version of intensive care, but she'll be out of here later in the day. Go on in."

"Thank you again." Eric grasped his hand and shook it enthusiastically. "You've done a great job."

The soldier smiled. "She's waiting for you."

Eric slipped into the cubicle and peered at the small form

lying under a white sheet. Several tubes ran out of her body. She looked pale but was breathing okay.

"Simone?"

Her eyes opened slowly. For a moment, she looked dazed; then she focused. "We're alive," she whispered. "Rather unbelievable, isn't it?"

Eric nodded. "Yeah."

"You saved my life. I would've been dead if it hadn't been for you." She reached out for his hand. "You got me off that beach and kept me alive. Do you have any idea what that means to me?"

"As you would say, 'Just doing my duty.'"

"I wanted you to leave me behind and you wouldn't." Tears welled up in her eyes. "I owe my life to you."

"Just knowing you're alive means everything to me."

"They tell me that I'm going to live in spite of having a couple of new holes in my body."

"I know. I'm so thankful."

She was quiet a moment. "But I have some things that I must tell you. After you know the truth, you may feel differently about me."

Eric squeezed her hand. "Simone, you don't have to—"

"Eric, we manipulated you from the beginning. Mossad knew you would never agree to do what we needed to accomplish, so we put you in a bind to force you to comply."

"I don't understand."

"There was no CIA or American government attempt to put you in prison. Gathering unauthorized intelligence information is a crime, but no one ever intended to charge you with that offense. We sent email messages that George Powers intercepted to make you think the Washington politicians were coming after you. They never were. I was the one who came up with this plan. You can blame me for the fear and chaos we created."

Eric blinked several times, not knowing what to say.

"We're also the ones who hacked into your Swiss bank account because we needed to know what resources you had for the assignments I had in mind. I was simply checking you out. Actually, I had several alternative plans that we might have tried. The other options would have been more expensive. We also found out that you have other bank accounts floating around."

Eric could hardly comprehend what she was telling him; he had never felt so outmaneuvered.

"Dar Dagan and I put this entire scheme together. Deception is an art. You know how the intelligence game is played. The nation of Israel had a mission of paramount importance, and we used the Conundrum to achieve our objective."

Simone had boxed him into a corner and won in a game that he never even realized they were playing. Seldom did anyone defeat him so completely.

Simone wiped away a tear running down her cheek. "I'm sorry," she said. "I know I pushed you away and treated you terribly on the freighter. I had to. The Sabbath night when I lit the candles, I realized that my heart had outrun my head. Honestly, I felt terribly confused, because I was falling in love with you. But I had pledged my life to the security of my country. I didn't know what to do, but my missions have always come first. I could finish the task only by pushing you away." Simone started to cry quietly. "I'm sorry, so sorry." Her tears poured down. "I didn't want to hurt you."

"Did you say you're falling in love with me?"

Simone nodded her head. "I guess I don't know how to show you. But yes, I am."

He could hardly breathe. "You *really* are?"

"I know it's over now," Simone said. "But it doesn't stop for me." She looked away with tears streaming down her cheeks. "I simply had to tell you the truth."

Eric reached down and gently pulled her chin back toward him. "Simone, I'm not ready to throw in the towel. It hurts my pride that you outsmarted us, but my hat's off to you. I could see us making great partners."

"Honestly? You mean that we might still have a future?"

"Look. We've discussed our differences before, and we still haven't worked through all of them. I know the fact that I'm a Gentile is no small issue for you and your people. Our worlds have considerable distance between them, but I'm still trying to build a bridge. Haven't given up on that task at all." He hugged her.

"Oh, Eric. I don't know where all of this is going, but I'm so glad you're still on the trail with me."

"Absolutely." Eric bent over and kissed her tenderly. "I think we're about to begin the greatest adventure of our lives. I don't know where we'll end up, but we certainly will find out together. Tomorrow will bring us another mountain to climb."

Simone kissed him again. "I've got my boots on."

AUTHOR'S NOTE

All characters, incidents, and situations in this story are purely fictional and have no relationship to any person living or dead. However, this story arises from incidents that actually happened. Behind *Network of Deception* lies an equally fascinating factual account of how the nuclear ambitions of Iran were frustrated through electronic intervention.

The *International Jerusalem Post* newspaper account of January 21–27, 2011, described a great number of Iranian email messages attempting to contact Tofino Security, believing they were involved in the creation of Stuxnet, a virus, worm, or malware suspected of severely damaging Iran's nuclear facilities. Many journalistic accounts described Stuxnet's effectiveness as the equivalent of a military attack. President Mahmoud Ahmadinejad admitted that Stuxnet had severely damaged the Natanz facility. When international inspectors visited the Natanz facility in 2009, they found nearly a thousand centrifuges had been shut down, resulting in speculation they had been disabled. While no nation admitted to causing the attack, credit was generally given to Israel and the United States. These accounts provided the basis for *Network of Deception*.

In fact, the Stuxnet code had the capacity to distort frequency converter drives used to control motors by changing the frequencies until the machines burned themselves out. Experts believe specially crafted USB drives accomplished such a task in Iran. The unique code caused the centrifuges to speed up while the monitoring computers reported no change in velocity. The devices destroyed themselves. These machines were used to enrich uranium and plutonium to a level used in creating bombs. By connecting with one computer in the Natanz network, the virus would automatically download and spread. The *Jerusalem Post* reported that the complexity of the Stuxnet device would have required five or six technicians to develop its deadly capacities.

Israel has also been suspected because of the code Stuxnet carried. One of the files in the device used the name Myrtus, a possible reference to Hadassah, the birth name of Jewish Queen Esther. An additional clue was the number 19790509 in the code, which could refer to the date that an important Persian Jew was executed on May 9, 1979, in Tehran.

In addition, the *New York Times*'s January 23, 2011, edition ran a story on former CIA agent Duane R. Clarridge, who started his own private spy agency because of discontent with the CIA. The story described Clarridge's disappointment with how the national agency functioned. This story provided the idea that became Eric Stone's Conundrum Agency.

The *New York Times* and the *Jerusalem Post* furnished the

backdrop for the "network" adventures. During my years of travel in Israel, I met people who supplied the ingredients in the character of Simone. They remain anonymous but deeply appreciated. My time spent in kibbutzim imparted the deepest appreciation for the price paid to create a powerful nation out of desert sand and through the efforts of dispossessed citizens fleeing Europe. A year ago, I sat in the Independence Hall in Tel Aviv, where David Ben-Gurion proclaimed the birth of Israel on May 14, 1948. As the *Jerusalem Post* reported, "a few hours later, Palestine was invaded by Muslim armies from the south, east, and north." Sitting in Independence Hall with the picture of Theodor Herzl in the center of two draped Israeli flags, I again realized how vital the security of the nation of Israel remains. My hope would be that this book further promotes that cause.

Spencer E. Moses is the pen name for a prolific author of both fiction and nonfiction. His writings have also been published in *Guidepost* books, as well as *Christianity Today*. He is a member of the Writer's Guild of New York City and served as senior vice president of Feed the Children. In addition, he is an archbishop in The Communion of Evangelical Episcopal churches. He lives in Colorado.